THE TINGLER UNLEASHED

The Tingler Unleashed

ISBN: 979-8-9886823-3-2 (hardback)
         979-8-9886823-4-9 (paperback)

Printed in the United States of America

THE TINGLER UNLEASHED

GARY J. ROSE

DEDICATION

Once more, I extend this book's dedication to my
sister, Debbie Miller. She has assumed the role of
the primary manuscript reader, a position once held
by our late mother, now watching over us from the
realms above. With her meticulous initial perusal,
she has skillfully unearthed numerous errors that had
eluded my discerning gaze.

I also offer this dedication to those belonging to the
'baby boomer' generation, individuals who frequented
the cinemas to experience the now delightfully kitschy
horror and science fiction films that both entertained
and frightened us. Devoid of the contemporary
marvels of special effects, they still managed to
seize our attention, evoking tense emotions as the
'monstrous' entities intricately wove their malevolent
pandemonium upon the silver screen.

May you derive immense pleasure from this
modern reinterpretation of William Castle's classic,
"The Tingler."

PROLOGUE

In the shadowy realms of the past, a terrifying tale emerged—a bone-chilling horror film known as "The Tingler." Produced and directed by the late William Castle, a master of fright behind iconic works like "House on Haunted Hill," this movie marked the third of five eerie collaborations between Castle and the renowned actor, Vincent Price.

Within the gripping narrative, a brilliant scientist named Dr. Warren Chapin makes a ghastly revelation—a parasite lurking in the human psyche, dubbed the "tingler," a creature that feeds on fear. This spine-chilling organism earned its eerie moniker by inducing a tingling sensation in its host's spine whenever terror seized them. In true Castle fashion, the film was accompanied by gimmicks to intensify the audience's experience, most notably the infamous "Percepto!" vibrating device strategically placed in select theater chairs.

On a fateful day in the United States, July 19, 1959, "The Tingler" hit the silver screens, eliciting a range of mixed reviews. Yet, over time, the film underwent critical reevaluation, eventually achieving the status of a beloved cult classic.

The story begins with Dr. Chapin's extraordinary discovery—a mysterious creature nestled along the human spine, the dreaded tingler. Whenever fear grips its host, the tingler thrives, feeding on terror until it can crush the spine entirely. However, it's devastating reign can be thwarted by one potent weapon—the primal scream.

In the heart of the chilling plot, movie theater owner Oliver Higgins, known for showcasing silent films, forms an unlikely connection with Dr. Chapin. But their camaraderie takes a harrowing turn when strange and supernatural events unfold, leading to the frightful demise of Higgins' wife, Martha. Trapped in silence due to her deafness and muteness, she falls prey to the tingler's relentless terror.

As Dr. Chapin unravels the sinister secret behind Martha's death and endeavors to contain the malevolent creature, the horrors of the past return with a vengeance. Revealing a dark and twisted truth, the true nature of Higgins is unveiled, exposing him as a murderer who heartlessly frightened his wife to her untimely end, knowing her inability to scream would seal her fate.

In a nightmarish turn of events, the tingler escapes its confines and embarks on a chilling rampage within Higgins' theater. It latches onto an unsuspecting woman's leg, and only her piercing scream grants her reprieve. Dr. Chapin must now confront the tingler head-on, devising a desperate plan to capture the creature once more and restore order.

In an eerie twist, Dr. Chapin realizes that the only way to neutralize the tingler is to reinsert it into Martha's lifeless body. As he carries out this unsettling task, the malevolent forces of the tingler begin to stir once more. Trapped within the theater, Higgins faces an unimaginable horror, and as the chilling climax unfolds, the boundaries between reality and the supernatural fray beyond recognition.

As the screen fades to darkness, Dr. Chapin's haunting voice echoes a final warning to the audience, urging them to confront their own tinglers that lie dormant within. But the film's unanswered questions and unresolved mysteries continue to linger in the hearts of those who dared to witness the terror.

Now, decades after the final credits rolled, the legacy of "The Tingler" resurfaces in a new reimagined and contemporary form—a novel that fast-forwards several years after the film's supposed conclusion. A fresh attempt to delve deeper into the tale and explore the lingering horrors that await. In this updated narrative, the tingler's malevolence returns, testing the limits of courage and unleashing the true essence of terror upon a new generation. Brace yourself as you embark on this hair-raising journey—the chilling saga of "The Tingler Unleashed" awaits.

FORWARD

In the eerie aftermath of the events that unfolded in the summer of 1959, the world believed they had seen the last of the dreaded "Tingler," a chilling creature that fed on fear, terrorizing the human spine. But history has a way of revisiting us, and now, decades later, darkness reawakens, and the tingler returns in all its spine-tingling glory.

Nestled in the embrace of misty mountains and ensconced by an eerie silence, Raven's Hollow seemed like any other picturesque small town on the surface. The cobblestone streets wound their way past cozy cottages and quaint shops, a movie theater that prided itself on showing silent movies, and townspeople bustling about, seemingly oblivious to the darkness that lurked beneath their idyllic facade.

But beneath the tranquility lay a long history of inexplicable happenings. Locals whispered in hushed tones about the unexplainable disappearances that occurred every year, leaving behind nothing but an empty void in the hearts of their loved ones.

Superstition clung to the air like an oppressive fog, as the townspeople refused to speak openly about the curse that seemed to haunt Raven's Hollow.

In the annals of spine-chilling tales, there was one legend that sent shivers down the spines of all who dared to listen - the haunting tale of The Tingler. It was many decades ago when a modest local movie house dared to screen a horror film that changed the course of history. As the terrifying creature materialized on the silver screen, an inexplicable horror gripped the unsuspecting audience.

To their astonishment, The Tingler seemed to transcend the boundaries of celluloid reality, stepping into the realm of the theater itself. With a malevolent intent, it viciously targeted a hapless female among the spectators, leaving the entire town bewildered and paralyzed with fear. The harrowing events of that fateful night etched an indelible mark in the minds of those who bore witness to the eerie encounter with The Tingler.

Amidst this unsettling atmosphere, the town of Raven's Hollow was about to experience an inexplicable threat like never before. Decades after the terrifying events at the movie house, two ambitious scientists led by Dr. Adrian Sinclair, arrived in town. Their goal was to continue the tingler experiments of Dr. Chapin and his assistant.

CHAPTER

ONE

C HIEF SARAH MORGAN, a distinguished
detective with a trailblazing career at the
LAPD, etched her name in history as the first
female police chief of Raven's Hallow, a quaint town.
After amassing accolades and honors, she chose to
venture away from the politically charged environment
of the big city's police department, seeking what she
hoped would be a serene and fulfilling role, guiding
her towards a peaceful retirement.

At the pinnacle of her 50th birthday, she defied
age with her impressive physical condition, a result
of quitting smoking years ago and maintaining a
dedicated morning workout routine. Towering at 5'8",
she effortlessly commanded attention the moment
she graced any room. Her luxuriously long, jet-black
hair exuded a radiant shine in the sunlight, capturing
the gaze of all who laid eyes on her. Accentuating her
allure were her deep, captivating dark brown eyes,

rendering her a truly striking and captivating woman at first sight.

As one approached her, the visible signs of aging became apparent, etched on her face by the weight of numerous years spent in law enforcement, with a significant portion dedicated to the demanding homicide division. The toll of stress and experience became evident, telling a story of dedication and sacrifice in the line of duty.

Only those who truly knew Sarah understood the immense tragedy she had endured—the heart-wrenching loss that had left her emotionally guarded and withdrawn. The merciless slaying of her beloved husband and daughter that had been inflicted by a cold-blooded serial killer, a malevolent presence whose trail Sarah had been relentlessly pursuing.

The pain of this unfathomable loss had seared her soul, leaving her hesitant to expose her heart to others, for she feared that embracing emotions could only lead to deeper anguish and sorrow. The scars of that fateful day had left her heart cocooned in protective armor, a fortress shielding her from the vulnerability of love and connection.

As a result, many people perceived her as cold and calculating, unable to see past the walls she had erected to shield herself from further heartbreak. Chief Morgan's stoic demeanor and reserved nature were a defense mechanism she had developed to cope with the profound grief that still lingered within her.

But beneath that exterior lay a woman whose heart had been shattered, struggling to find the strength to heal and trust again.

She arrived at the quaint police station in the heart of Raven's Hallow, punctual as always. Her initial encounter with the town had been during a meeting with the mayor and city council who were considering her for the chief's position. She couldn't help but marvel at the picturesque charm of Raven's Hallow. The cozy ambiance, with its snow-covered streets and charming buildings, had struck her as the perfect backdrop for a heartwarming Hallmark movie set during the magical Christmas season. Little did she know that behind this idyllic facade lay a town with secrets and mysteries waiting to be unraveled.

As she stepped into the station, a bell announced her entrance. A warm and welcoming smile greeted Chief Morgan. A young woman with long, flowing blonde hair stood by her desk, seemingly engrossed in her cell phone, a sight quite common in the generations that followed Sarah's. "Hello Chief Morgan, I'm Sandy, the daytime desk officer. It's a pleasure to finally meet you," she said with genuine enthusiasm in her voice. Despite the digital distraction, Sandy's cheerful demeanor and friendly attitude shone through, making Chief Morgan feel a sense of comfort in her new surroundings.

Sarah extended her hand for a handshake, and Sandy appeared slightly taken aback by the formality of the gesture. Nevertheless, she reciprocated the handshake warmly. "Nice to meet you too, Sandy. Now, could you please show me where my office is?" Chief Morgan inquired.

"Oh, it's right back here. The place is so small you can't get lost," Sandy cheerfully replied, leaving her desk to guide Sarah down a brief hallway. "Here's the bathroom. It's a co-ed facility, so just remember to knock before entering," she explained with a helpful tone, ensuring that Chief Morgan was familiar with the station's layout from the get-go.

As they continued the brief tour, Chief Morgan couldn't help but appreciate Sandy's amiable nature and willingness to assist in settling her into the tight-knit community of Raven's Hallow.

As Sarah stepped into the room, Sandy held the door open and entered behind her. "The place is just as it was when Chief Callahan was here," Sandy remarked with a hint of nostalgia in her voice. "He passed away from a heart attack a few weeks ago. This station meant the world to him; it was like his second home." Her tone became somber as she continued, "It's a shame he had no family. Only his officers and the townspeople attended his funeral to pay their respects."

In that moment, Chief Morgan sensed the weight of the legacy she was stepping into. She could feel the lingering presence of Chief Callahan, and the realization of the tight-knit bond he had with the station and the community left her with a sense of responsibility to honor his memory and continue his legacy in Raven's Hallow.

Sarah inquired as she settled into her seat, "I comprehend that the department is composed of five officers. Is that information accurate?" During my interview, I posed the same question, but the Mayor merely mentioned that the department had sufficient staff."

"It seems like something Sam would say. Though he holds the position of the mayor, many folks here view him as somewhat untrustworthy. Perhaps I shouldn't have expressed it that way, but that's the prevailing sentiment among the people in this area."

"By Sam, do you mean Mr. Wadsworth?" Sarah asked.

"Yeah, that's the one, old money bags himself. His family comes from generations of wealth. Back in the 1800s, this entire region thrived on silver mining, and up there (she gestured towards the mountains), they struck a significant silver deposit, leading to a bonanza. That's how Raven's Hollow was founded. Sam's family owned and operated the largest mine, and before the mines ran dry, the Wadsworth's amassed a fortune. As a result, he now holds mortgages on most of the downtown buildings," Sandy said.

"Hmm," Sarah pondered for a moment. "Sandy, is there any coffee available nearby? I could really use a cup right now."

"Yes, Chief, we have some. As a matter of fact, one of the first things I do each morning is brew a few pots. It's mainly for the day shift officers since the graveyard shift just wants to head home and get some rest. Would you like me to bring you a cup? How do you take your coffee?"

"That's okay. Lead me to the breakroom." Sarah stood and walked towards the door. "So, are you one of my officers?"

"No, I wish I was. Currently, I'm attending the community college, working towards earning my Associate Degree in Criminal Justice by next fall. My ultimate dream is to become a detective someday. However, it's unlikely to happen here, given the town's small size and lack of funds for new positions," Sandy replied.

"Never say never," Sarah encouraged. "I'm not sure how much the mayor shared about my background with the department, but before I came here, I was a homicide investigator with the Los Angeles Police Department."

"Really?" Sandy exclaimed excitedly as they arrived at the breakroom, a small converted closet with a Bunn coffee maker and styrofoam cups filled with sugar, sugar substitutes, and powdered cream. "I'd love to learn from you about what it takes for a woman to become a detective. A homicide detective from the LAPD? That's so exciting!"

Sarah smiled warmly at Sandy's enthusiasm. "It's great to see your passion. Becoming a detective takes dedication, training, and experience. We can talk more about it during our break, and I'll be happy to share some insights from my time at the Los Angeles Police Department."

Sarah spotted a clean cup and made a mental note to bring her own cup from home, which she currently resided in—a charming bed-and-breakfast place situated on the outskirts of the main street. The place exuded a quaint ambiance, reminiscent of a picturesque setting for another Hallmark romance movie. While the bed-and-breakfast offered both breakfast and dinner, Sarah had left early this morning, way before the other guests were even awake. Depending on how her first day on the job went, she would decide whether to have dinner there or not.

Sarah and Sandy sat together in the Chief's office, sharing a cup of coffee. As the conversation flowed, Sarah began to feel more at ease in her new work environment. "So, Sandy," she said thoughtfully, "I suppose I'll be relying on you to bring me up to speed. With five officers, including you, how did the previous chief allocate the manpower?"

"Well, things were relatively manageable until someone fell sick. That's when it gets dicey. That Covid shit really hit us hard, but eventually, we started seeing it more like a common flu that the media, as usual, blew out of proportion. The chief considered himself as one of the officers. He, along with Officer Mary Ellen Staton, covered the day shift from 0800 to 1600 hours. If you'd like, we can head to the briefing room, and I can create a chart to help you get a better understanding of our manpower distribution."

In the briefing room, which was roughly the same size as Sarah's office, a large whiteboard adorned the wall. To Sarah's surprise, someone had posted the odds for that weekend's NFL games, prompting her to raise an eyebrow. Sandy noticed her reaction and swiftly moved to erase the board, clearing any distractions from the room.

Sandy took a marker and started writing on the whiteboard. "Alright, for the day shift from 0800 to 1600 hours, we have the Chief and Officer Mary Ellen Statton. Moving on to the swing shift, which goes from 1600 to 2400 hours, Officers Tim Moore and Dan Stansberry handle the responsibilities. It seems like most of the action occurs during the swing shift. During the graveyard shift, from 2400 to 0800 hours, Officer Paul Kneale takes charge. And lastly, we have the Flex Officer, Officer Carl Thompson, who covers days off, sick calls, and fills in as needed."

"Man, that's tight coverage for a population of just under 55,000. In my opinion, we should at least double our manpower to ensure effective policing," Sarah remarked.

Sandy nodded in agreement. "You're absolutely right, but Chief Callahan had a tough time convincing the mayor and the city council to provide additional funds. He would return here after each meeting, having been shot down once again, and vent his frustration by swearing and shouting until he ran out of energy," Sandy chuckled at the memory of Chief Callahan's passionate responses.

Sarah glanced at her watch which showed 7:35. "When does Officer Statton come in and the graveyard officer, what is his name, Officer Kneale normally call it a night?"

On cue, the two heard the front office bell activate and the two left Sarah's office to go upfront. In walked a fully uniformed Officer Mary Ellen Statton.

CHAPTER

TWO

"CHIEF MORGAN, I'D like you to meet our day shift officer, Mary Ellen Statton," Sandy introduced. Mary Ellen stood at 5'7", with collar-length brown hair, showing a touch of gray, and perhaps carrying an extra ten pounds, which she discreetly tried to conceal by sucking in her gut as she extended her hand to Sarah.

"Wow, a female Chief of Police. Raven's Hallow is finally stepping into the modern age. It's a pleasure to meet you, Chief," Mary Ellen greeted with a warm smile.

"Likewise, Mary Ellen. I heard from Sandy that we'll be holding down the fort together from 0800 to 1600 hours. I'm excited to work with you and get to know the town better. Starting tomorrow, I'll be riding along with you so you can show me the lay of the land and get me acquainted with everything. Before you head out, I do have a question," Sarah continued. "Can you and Sandy join me back in the briefing room? There's something I'd like to discuss regarding the manpower that I now want to address."

Once they entered the briefing room, Mary Ellen's eyes immediately caught sight of the list of officers, including her name, and noticed the absence of the NFL odds. Though she didn't mention it, Sarah keenly observed her reaction.

"Here's my question," Sarah began, directing their attention to the board. "On days like today, we have you, me, and Sandy at the front desk for the day shift. Assuming we all work Monday through Friday, who covers the front office and patrols the streets during the weekends and holidays?"

Before anyone could respond, Sarah continued, pointing at the board. "I understand we have Officer Thompson as our flex officer, but there's only so much he can cover. And I didn't even address the shortages that must occur during everyone's vacation. I need some help ladies in figuring this out."

Sandy deferred to Mary Ellen, who wore a big grin, eagerly anticipating the chance to explain to Sarah. "Well, Chief, on weekends, we actually close up the office and place a sign on the front door stating that we are closed and listing your phone number to call for emergencies. As for the other shortages you mentioned, Chief Callahan used to cover extra shifts by himself, and there were occasions when we ran the swing shift with just one officer instead of two." Mary Ellen noticed the look of shock on Sarah's face before she continued.

"A few months ago, before Chief Callahan passed away, swing shift was down to one man since Officer Moore was home in bed with the Chinese flu. To make matters worse, there was a fatal accident out on Route 81 that tied up Officer Stansberry for hours, leaving the calls for service to pile up until the graveyard shift or even onto the dayshift. Welcome to Raven's Hallow," Mary Ellen's voice carried a hint of bitterness.

"Well, I can already sense my first battle with Mayor Wadsworth," Sarah said, her tone tinged with dejection as she tried to hide her sadness.

"Good luck with that," Mary Ellen replied. "I personally feel that Chief Callahan died from a heart attack brought on by his continuing battle with, quote, His Honor."

"Well, I wonder if His Honor has heard of unsafe workplace lawsuits? I think that a multi-million dollar suit against the town would quickly get the attention of the city council," Sarah contemplated.

"Oh, I like your thinking, Chief," Mary Ellen said with a hint of admiration. She finished getting her gear together before heading out to hit the streets. "Look forward to you riding along tomorrow. See you later, Sandy." With that, Sarah and Sandy watched Mary Ellen check out her patrol car and drive off down Main Street.

Sarah addressed Sandy, instructing her on her first assignment. "Please follow your usual protocol for now and inform all the troops about a mandatory meeting tomorrow afternoon at 3 pm. We'll be gathering in the briefing room, or whatever we can call it. This will give the graveyard officer, either Kneale or Thompson, whoever is on duty tonight, a chance to get a few hours of sleep before attending the meeting."

"Sandy sheepishly asked the Chief, 'Chief, is this for overtime?' "Absolutely," the Chief replied, "Why do you ask?"

"Well, whenever Chief Callahan approved overtime, the mayor would go ballistic and deny it," Sandy explained.

"That's ridiculous. People don't work for free. I wonder what the United States Department of Labor said about that?"

"It never got that far. Chief Callahan would just pay the overtime out of his own pocket to appease the mayor."

"Really? Well, there is the second bone I will have to fight over with Mr. Mayor. In fact, please make sure when you alert the staff that, due to the meeting being mandatory, overtime has been authorized."

Mayor Samuel "Sam" Wadsworth was a man of substantial girth, with a short stature and receding hairline. To compensate for his physical appearance, he spared no expense on his attire, donning exquisitely tailored designer suits, luxurious silk shirts, and stylish ties. In his pursuit to make a lasting impression on others, he indulged in smoking Cohiba Behike cigars, each costing a staggering $450. These prized cigars found a home in a custom-made humidor crafted from cherrywood, adorned with his initials in gold, and prominently displayed on his grand 12' mahogany desk.

With an air of arrogance and self-importance, Mayor Samuel "Sam" Wadsworth glanced at his watch and noted that it was almost 10 am, time for what he believed to be the most crucial meeting of his life. His office door was intentionally left open, allowing him to hear and see his secretary, Amanda, diligently typing away at her desk. Before summoning her, he stared at her model-like body and indulged in a brief, conceited daydream of himself in bed with her, as if he were a deity entitled to such fantasies.

"Amanda!" he bellowed imperiously. "Get in here immediately!"

Amanda obediently rose from her seat, pulling down her black short skirt, and entered the mayor's office. The Mayor, in his self-centered mindset, relished the sight of Amanda adjusting her attire, convinced that it was a deliberate act of teasing, orchestrated solely for his gratification.

"Yes, Mr. Mayor," Amanda responded dutifully as she positioned herself in front of the mayor's desk.

Wadsworth's response was delayed, his gaze fixated on Amanda's chest, where the fabric revealed a glimpse of her black bra. Feeling uneasy and without hesitation, Amanda quickly pulled a chair across from the mayor, obstructing his attempt to look under her skirt, attempting to preserve some semblance of professionalism in the uncomfortable situation.

"As you're aware, Mr. Shields and his attorneys representing Dreamscape will arrive promptly at 10:00. I expect you to have everything prepared, including coffee and pastries to be served once they are seated."

"Yes, Sir. Sweetway Bakery will be delivering the pastries any minute, and I have a fresh pot of coffee ready in the break room. I'll bring it in as soon as everyone is settled."

"Understood. Amanda, while I expect a high level of professionalism, it's essential for you to show a bit more warmth and ease during the meeting. This opportunity with Dreamscape holds great significance for Raven's Hollow. If they choose to launch their groundbreaking virtual reality technology here, our tax revenue will soar, leading to more jobs and improved pay for our employees. Your friendly demeanor will play a vital role in this, as we want them to feel welcome and eager to invest in our town."

The two of them heard a commotion from the neighboring office, signaling the arrival of the pastry company. Amanda promptly got up from her chair and headed out to welcome them, while the Mayor's gaze uncomfortably lingered on her figure as she walked away.

"Oh, and another thing. Call Chief Morgan and tell her to come to my office tomorrow morning at 8 AM sharp," Wadsworth instructed his secretary.

From his window, Wadsworth saw a white stretch limo arrive in the city's parking lot. The driver hurried to open the side door, but an occupant had already partially opened it. Eventually, three sharply attired men, two white and one black, stepped out of the vehicle, each carrying a briefcase. They strode confidently toward the large government building.

"They're here. They're here," Wadsworth announced to Amanda. He closed the door to his office, straightened his tie, and rearranged objects on his desk for the umpteenth time while relighting his cigar. Eager to make a good impression, he strained to hear Amanda exchanging greetings with the representatives of Dreamscape and offering them seats.

Soon, Wadsworth opened his door and saw the three individuals sitting. "Amanda, why didn't you tell me these gentlemen have arrived? Please come in. Amanda, please bring some coffee and refreshments."

The three individuals stood up and walked into the mayor's office, with two of them smiling at Amanda. However, as soon as she turned her back to them, she slyly flipped them her middle finger while walking towards the break room.

As the three sharply attired representatives from Dreamscape settled into their seats, Mayor Wadsworth tried to exude an air of confidence and charm. He envisioned this meeting as a crucial opportunity to convince them that Raven's Hallow was the ideal location for their Virtual Reality plant and theatre.

"Welcome, gentlemen, to the beautiful town of Raven's Hallow," Wadsworth began with a practiced smile. "I must say, your company's reputation in the Virtual Reality industry precedes you, and I firmly believe that our city offers the perfect setting for your ambitious venture."

The first representative, Mr. Thomas, a seasoned executive with a warm demeanor, leaned forward, nodding in appreciation. "We're delighted to be here, Mayor Wadsworth. Your town does hold a certain charm. However, we must consider various factors before making such a significant investment."

Wadsworth nodded eagerly, eager to address their concerns. "Of course, of course. Allow me to highlight a few key aspects that make Raven's Hallow an excellent choice. Firstly, our town's proximity to major highways and transportation hubs ensures convenient accessibility for your clientele. Additionally, we have a thriving tech-savvy community that could contribute to the success of your venture." There was a slight knock on the mayor's door, followed by its opening.

Amanda gracefully entered the room, pushing a large serving tray adorned with an assortment of delectable pastries. A hot coffee carafe, along with sugar, cream, and two plates of freshly baked treats, completed the ensemble. "Thank you, Amanda," Mayor Wadsworth said with a nod of appreciation.

As the three representatives savored the sight of the enticing refreshments, Wadsworth couldn't help but notice their admiration of Amanda's appearance.

The second representative, Mr. Rodriguez, a shrewd negotiator, leaned back in his chair, assessing the mayor's pitch. "Indeed, accessibility and local talent are essential, but we also need a location with a certain appeal to the masses. What unique offerings does Raven's Hallow bring to the table?"

Wadsworth was quick to respond, his excitement evident. "Ah, you see, our town boasts a rich history and captivating legends that can be brilliantly woven into your Virtual Reality experiences. Imagine the thrill of stepping into the shoes of our town's infamous folklore characters or exploring the mysterious haunted places that Raven's Hallow is known for. It's a golden opportunity to create immersive storytelling experiences that will enthrall your users."

The third representative, Mr. Nguyen, a soft-spoken engineer, interjected, "That sounds intriguing, Mayor Wadsworth. However, we also require state-of-the-art infrastructure and a supportive regulatory environment."

With unwavering enthusiasm, Wadsworth continued, "You'll find that Raven's Hallow is deeply committed to attracting innovative industries like yours. We have a dedicated team ready to assist with any infrastructure needs and a business-friendly regulatory framework that prioritizes growth and success."

The room fell silent as the representatives contemplated the mayor's pitch. After a moment, Mr. Thomas broke the silence with a smile. "Mayor Wadsworth, your passion for your city is evident, and we appreciate your vision. We will carefully evaluate all the factors before making a decision."

Wadsworth beamed with hope. "Thank you for considering Raven's Hallow. I'm confident that we can forge a fruitful partnership that benefits both Dreamscape and our town."

As the meeting progressed, the representatives asked more questions, delving into the finer details of the proposal. They exchanged business cards, promising to stay in touch. Mayor Wadsworth was left with a sense of optimism, hoping that his efforts would bear fruit and that Raven's Hallow would soon become home to the innovative Virtual Reality plant and theatre he had envisioned.

S ARAH'S CELL PHONE buzzed insistently on her nightstand, jolting her awake. Still disoriented from the move to Raven's Hollow, she fumbled around, trying to locate the source of the noise. Finally, her hand found the phone, and she noticed an unfamiliar number on the screen, reminding her that she was no longer in Los Angeles. *"Nothing good happens with a phone call at 4:00 in the morning."*

Taking a deep breath, she answered the call with a hint of uncertainty in her voice, "This is Chief Morgan. Can I help you?"

A calm voice on the other end identified itself as County Dispatch, relaying urgent news. "Hello, Chief. We have a situation. One of your officers is requesting your immediate response to the scene of a DB - dead body - on Route 81 near the crossing of Elks Point. Since you're new to Raven's Hollow, if you head to your station first, you can pick up a patrol car.

We'll send the vehicle the GPS coordinates to guide you there."

Sarah's eyebrows furrowed as she absorbed the information. "Thank you. That would be a great help. I should arrive at the station in approximately 15 minutes."

The dispatcher responded empathetically, "Not a problem, Chief. Sorry to start off your new job with a possible homicide." With a mix of determination and apprehension, Sarah ended the call, realizing that her second day as Chief of Police in Raven's Hollow was going to be far from ordinary.

Dressing swiftly in a pant suit, Sarah realized that once she freed herself from the scene, she needed to head to the station to continue her day. She pulled her hair back into a ponytail, giving herself a quick once-over before getting into her private car and driving to the station. Upon arrival, she recalled where the keys to the patrol vehicles were stored and discovered that three cars were still available. Grabbing all three sets of keys, she walked to the parking lot.

With a press of the key fob, the second vehicle responded with a chirp, indicating that it was the newest of the three. Deciding it was the best option, she walked towards it, leaving the other two sets of keys at the station's front desk and securing the front door. Settling into the patrol car, she adjusted her seat and fired up the engine, pleasantly surprised to find that the vehicle was equipped with a navigation system.

"Well, at least Mr. Mayor didn't skimp on adding some extras to the city's patrol vehicles," she remarked to herself with a wry smile. The dispatcher, whose name she never got, had indeed programmed the directions to the scene as promised. Sarah familiarized herself with the emergency equipment and activated the lights and siren before following the guidance provided by the navigation system.

As she rushed to the scene, her mind began to churn with questions about the case and the potential implications for her new position in Raven's Hollow. The urgency of the situation only intensified her determination.

After what felt like a good fifteen minutes, the flashing lights of her graveyard officer's vehicle came into view. As Sarah approached the scene, she tried to recall the names of the two possible officers who might be there. It was either Officer Kneale or the flex officer, Thompson. However, their first names seemed to elude her at the moment. She hoped that at the 3 PM meeting later that day, she would do a better job of putting faces to names and getting to know her team better.

Stepping out of the patrol car, Sarah was met by Officer Paul Kneale. He extended his hand with a friendly greeting, "Lousy way to impress our new Chief by calling her out of bed at 4:00 AM." They shook hands as she replied, "Goes with the territory. By the way, I apologize, but I can't recall your first name."

"It's Paul, Chief," he responded. Paul then pointed to an older man standing nearby and introduced him as Dewey Parsons. "He was on his way to work at the dairy and came across the body."

As they approached Dewey, Sarah observed that he seemed to be suffering from osteoporosis. "My God. He gets up every morning at 4 AM at his age to do what, milk the cows?"

"Yep," Paul confirmed. "He and his brother Ennis run a large dairy farm about four miles from here on Route 79. Can't miss the place due to the smell." He chuckled before continuing. "Anyway, Dewey spotted the body in the middle of the road, and he pulled over. He put out some flares, but as you can see, no one else is out and about at this hour."

Upon reaching the body, Sarah saw an elderly woman lying face down, wearing what appeared to be a hospital gown. "Huh. Does Raven's Hollow have a hospital?"

"No, Chief. We have a 24/7 Urgent Care about eight miles away on the other side of town," Paul explained.

Kneeling down for a closer look at the victim's face, Sarah noticed something peculiar. "There's something strange about her face, but we'll get a better view once the coroner arrives. Have you called them yet?"

"No, Chief. I wanted to wait until you got here. Should I make the call now?" Paul asked.

"I'm not entirely familiar with the area's protocols yet, but let's go ahead and request the coroner's response. I'd like to get the investigation moving. And if you've already taken Mr. Parsons' statement, you can let him go back to his cows. I'm sure they can't wait for him," she added with a smile, hoping to lighten the grim atmosphere.

The coroner and her male assistant did not arrive until an hour and forty-five minutes later. It was almost 6 AM and a little more traffic started to occupy the road. New flares were put out and Sarah and Officer Kneale directed traffic as necessary. Arriving in a white county van marked with "Coroner's Office" on the sides stopped just before the flare pattern.

Dr. Chelsea Lawrence was a mid-forties, average height and weight, white female, sporting a shoulder length brunette hairdo. She and her assistant were already wearing some protective clothing and put on their disposable gloves while walking up to Sarah and Kneale.

"Not an ideal way to meet the new Chief of Police of Raven's Hallow. I'm Chelsea Lawrence. Nice to meet you. And this is my sidekick, Jamal Reddy," Chelsea introduced herself and her companion. After exchanging pleasantries, Sarah provided Chelsea with some background information.

"Well, Chief, I can tell you just from what the victim is wearing that you have your first homicide," Chelsea said with a somber tone.

"Please, call me Sarah. You have me at an obvious disadvantage, Doctor. How can you determine it is a homicide without examining the corpse?" Sarah inquired, genuinely curious.

Dr. Lawrence took a deep breath before responding, "First, call me Chelsea. I assume your mayor," she air-quoted the term to imply her skepticism about Wadsworth's transparency, "did not inform you about the recent disappearances that have occurred over the past several years throughout the county, with a few in Raven's Hallow."

"You're correct Chelsea. The mayor never covered that among other things. I have a meeting with him this morning and have a few things to discuss." She extended a smile showing her resolve about Wadsworth already.

"Alright. Let's get to it," Dr. Lawrence said as her assistant was already taking photographs of the scene and victim. "You got all the shots, Jamal? Make sure you bag her hands just in case we get lucky with some trace evidence. We'll print her when we get her back to the office."

"Yes, Doctor," he responded standing close to the body realizing that soon he would be requested to turn the corpse over.

Retrieving a mini-microphone from her protective pants, she began her examination. "The deceased is a white female, with an approximate age between mid-seventies and eighties. The body is in a face-down position, with her head turned to the right, revealing the dental region. She appears to possess her natural teeth, and no partial dentures are visibly present. An autopsy will be necessary to confirm this. The clothing worn by the deceased resembles a hospital gown. There's noticeable blood around the spinal area, though no blood is visible on other regions of the body. It appears that the gown is the only garment being worn by the deceased. I don't see any other objects on the body nor in the surrounding area; No purse, no cell phone."

"The body exhibits signs of rigor mortis, indicating that the individual has been deceased for several hours. However, it seems that the body has been repositioned, as the rigor is observed on the incorrect side of the corpse."

With great care, she gingerly raises the hospital gown, revealing the shocking discovery of the victim's spleen had been removed. "The victim's spine appears to have been deliberately extracted through surgical means," she stated, her voice conveying the gravity of the situation. "Considering the significant blood saturation on the gown, a potential cause of death could be exsanguination, possibly combined with shock if the victim was not under general anesthesia during the procedure."

Recognizing the need to preserve the victim's dignity, she gently pulled the gown back down, granting the deceased a semblance of modesty during this distressing examination.

She glances towards Jamal to signal that she would like the body to be turned over for further examination.

Sarah and Officer Kneale were taken aback as they first laid eyes on the face of the deceased. Her eyes were wide open, appearing almost bulging out of their sockets. The expression on her face seemed to be locked in a state of simultaneous fear and amusement, frozen in time. Her upper and lower lips had retracted, revealing both the upper and lower gum lines, adding to the unsettling appearance of the deceased.

Dr. Lawrence keenly observed the reactions of both Sarah and Officer Kneale. It was evident that the sight of the deceased had a profound impact on them. Officer Kneale wore a repulsed expression, struggling to suppress an urge to vomit. On the other hand, Sarah's curiosity and determination only grew stronger. She moved even closer to the body, fixating on the frozen and terrifying expression displayed by the elderly victim.

"Dr. Lawrence, I mean Chelsea, can you turn the body over again?"

"Sure." She nods at Jamal who started turning the corpse over. "Something specific you are looking for?"

Sarah carefully donned her protective gloves before lifting the hospital garment, directing her focus to the area around the spine. "Chelsea, you're the medical doctor, but I've encountered my fair share of cases involving violence. The removal of the spleen seems to have been done with surgical precision. Do you agree?"

Observing Sarah's expertise, Chelsea couldn't help but be impressed. Curiosity getting the best of her, she inquired, "Watching you work, Sarah, I can tell you've got experience. What's your background, if you don't mind me asking?"

With a hint of pride, Sarah replied, "Nineteen years with LAPD homicide."

Chelsea was genuinely impressed. "Wow. Wadsworth truly got a valuable asset for his city. You're absolutely right in your assessment. This method of removing the spleen matches how we found the other victims. All of them had their spleens surgically removed without causing harm to surrounding tissues or organs."

"I'd like to attend the post if that is possible?" Sarah asked. "And I like Officer Kneale to attend also."

"Not a problem. I'm going to train Officer Kneale into a homicide investigator?"

"That's how I got my start. When you anticipate conducting your post?"

"Things have been slow. Does 10 AM tomorrow morning work for you and your officer?" Sarah looked at Kneale who nodded.

"See you tomorrow morning at 10. Nice meeting you."

CHAPTER

FOUR

A S SARAH RETURNED to the police station after tending to the gruesome scene of the homicide, her sense of urgency battled with the need to clean up. A quick ten-minute delay found her stepping through the police station doors, freshly scrubbed but still running behind for her inaugural meeting with Mayor Wadsworth since assuming her new role. The encounter had its weight, for her appearance before the mayor held the potential to set the tone for her tenure in Raven' Hollow.

Navigating her way to the receptionist's area, Sarah was met with the welcoming face of Amanda, who manned the front desk with an air of practiced efficiency. "Hello, I'm Chief Sarah Morgan," Sarah introduced herself with a polite nod. "Nice to meet you."

As pleasantries exchanged in the midst of their meeting, the imposing door to the mayor's office swung open, revealing Mayor Wadsworth. His demeanor was far from jovial, his stern gaze flicking impatiently to his wristwatch as if time was a currency he couldn't afford to squander. "Chief, you're finally here," he chided with a hint of irritation, gesturing for Sarah to enter his inner sanctum. Without further ado, he pivoted and disappeared back into his office, the door clicking closed behind him.

Amanda and Sarah exchanged a fleeting smile, a touch of sarcasm coloring their expressions. "Welcome, Sarah," Amanda's voice carried an undertone of camaraderie. "Stay tough. He's mostly a paper tiger."

With those words hanging in the air, Sarah mentally braced herself for the meeting ahead. The mayor's stern reputation was no secret, and his impatience only reinforced the challenges she was here to face. As the door to the mayor's office beckoned, Sarah squared her shoulders and strode forward, ready to confront whatever awaited her within those walls.

"I hold my supervisory staff to a high standard of punctuality," Mayor Wadsworth's voice carried a stern edge as he addressed Sarah. His gaze, fixed on her, seemed to demand an explanation for her delayed arrival.

Sarah's response was unapologetically direct. "If you deem a homicide involving an eighty-year-old woman, her lifeless body discarded on Route 81, a suitable justification for my tardiness, then indeed, I do have a reason."

"Homicide," Mayor Wadsworth's initial sternness gave way to an unexpected shock. The weight of the revelation seemed to momentarily silence him. "Who is the victim? What transpired?" His questions tumbled forth, the mayor clearly unprepared for such a profound response from the newly appointed Chief. "Has the press made any attempts to contact you yet?" he inquired further, his concern palpable.

The exchange held an undercurrent of tension, a clash between the mayor's administrative expectations and the grim realities Sarah confronted in her role. As the weight of the situation settled in the room, it became clear that the horrors lurking in Raven' Hollow were pressing upon the boundaries of the everyday, demanding attention and action.

"The victim's identity is pending. The coroner is in the process of running her fingerprints, and I'm scheduled to witness the autopsy at 10 am tomorrow. Hopefully, by then, we'll have more information to work with and follow up on," Sarah explained, her tone measured as she detailed her plans.

Mayor Wadsworth reclined in his oversized executive leather chair, the weight of his authority evident even as he listened. "Are you certain this is a homicide? Perhaps it's a case of an unfortunate pedestrian accident on a poorly lit road," he mused, offering an alternative explanation.

Sarah's response was firm, carrying the weight of her years of experience. "Mr. Mayor, as you may recall, I spent nearly two decades as a homicide investigator with the LAPD. A victim whose spleen has been surgically removed doesn't suggest a casual stroll at 4 AM, let alone a simple accident involving a vehicle."

The mayor found himself momentarily taken aback by the depth of her expertise, a realization that surfaced as defensiveness in his expression. Sarah had put him on the defensive, highlighting the gap in their understanding of the situation. The mayor grappled with a twinge of regret, questioning whether his choice to hire someone who wouldn't be easily intimidated or manipulated was the right one after all.

"I see," Mayor Wadsworth's response came with a calculated air, revealing his inclination towards micromanagement. "When the press reaches out for a televised press release, I expect to be present for that interaction. Additionally, ensure that I'm cc'd on any written press releases as the case unfolds. I want to be kept in the loop as this progresses." Silence filled the room for a few seconds before it was broken by Wadsworth.

"Well, a belated welcome to Raven's Hollow, Chief Morgan," Mayor Wadsworth's voice took on a hint of warmth that seemed more perfunctory than genuine. "How are you finding our little town so far? I hope it's been a smooth transition for you." He leaned back in his chair, a practiced gesture intended to convey openness but perhaps slightly marred by the ever-present air of formality that clung to him.

"Raven's Hollow has its charms, no doubt," Sarah replied diplomatically, her tone respectful as she navigated the nuances of the conversation. "It's quite different from the city life I've been accustomed to. And as for the transition, well, I'm finding my way."

The mayor nodded, his eyes briefly scanning the room as if gauging its adequacy. "Good to hear. Just remember, Chief Morgan, my door is always open. If you have any concerns or need to discuss anything – be it department matters or even just thoughts about the town – don't hesitate to reach out."

"Thank you, Mayor," Sarah's response was measured, appreciative of the offer even as she sensed the underlying implications of his words. The delicate dance between autonomy and oversight was evident in their exchange.

Mayor Wadsworth's gaze fixed on Sarah, his expression one of mild scrutiny. "I have high expectations for this town, Chief. We're on the cusp of something significant with that Virtual Reality firm considering setting up shop here. A real game-changer for Raven's Hollow. I trust that you'll play your part in ensuring everything proceeds smoothly."

"Of course, Mayor," Sarah's tone was confident, acknowledging the weight of responsibility that lay ahead. "I'm committed to upholding the law and maintaining order in Raven's Hollow, especially during this pivotal time."

The mayor's lips curved into a thin smile, the satisfaction of control subtly present. "I have no doubt you'll manage just fine, Chief Morgan. Our paths will cross often, I'm sure. Now, if you'll excuse me, there's some preparation I need to attend to regarding that VR firm's meeting."

"Certainly, Mayor," Sarah replied, offering a nod of understanding. Feeling she had been summarily dismissed, she rose and walked out of his office. She had rethought about confronting the mayor about prior similar homicides in Raven's Hollow, feeling she should wait until she learned more from Dr. Lawrence and reviewed any files on the cases.

As Sarah turned to make her exit, a nagging sensation lingered in the back of her mind. Beneath the carefully constructed veneer of formality and politeness, she couldn't shake the feeling that an intricate web of power dynamics was silently weaving its threads through the heart of Raven's Hollow.

Stepping into her role as Chief, she realized, demanded a delicate balance: one where she navigated the currents of appeasing the mayor's preferences while unflinchingly pursuing justice on her own terms.

A soft voice pulled her attention as she walked past Amanda's desk. "I'm impressed," Amanda whispered, a hint of admiration lacing her words. "You didn't let that asshole get under your skin."

Sarah managed a small, knowing smile in response. "Thank you, Amanda. It's a skill I've had some practice with."

Amanda's eyes twinkled with a mix of sympathy and camaraderie. "Well, I hope you find your footing here and actually enjoy your new job. Maybe, once you're a bit more settled, we can grab lunch together. I could give you a bit of background information about His Highness," she added with a wry grin, her gaze pointed in the direction of the mayor's office.

Sarah's interest piqued, and she nodded appreciatively. "That sounds like a plan. Maybe sometime next week. I'll give you a call."

With that, Sarah headed out, her thoughts a mix of anticipation and intrigue. In a town where subtleties ran deep and the layers of power weren't always apparent at first glance, she was beginning to realize that forging alliances and gathering insights beyond the obvious could be just as crucial to her success as solving the mysteries that Raven's Hollow held.

Stepping into her role as Chief, she realized, demanded a delicate balance: one where she navigated the currents of appeasing the mayor's preferences while unflinchingly pursuing justice on her own terms.

A soft voice pulled her attention as she walked past Amanda's desk. "I'm impressed," Amanda whispered, a hint of admiration lacing her words. "You didn't let that asshole get under your skin."

Sarah managed a small, knowing smile in response. "Thank you, Amanda. It's a skill I've had some practice with."

Amanda's eyes twinkled with a mix of sympathy and camaraderie. "Well, I hope you find your footing here and actually enjoy your new job. Maybe, once you're a bit more settled, we can grab lunch together. I could give you a bit of background information about His Highness," she added with a wry grin, her gaze pointed in the direction of the mayor's office.

Sarah's interest piqued, and she nodded appreciatively. "That sounds like a plan. Maybe sometime next week. I'll give you a call."

With that, Sarah headed out, her thoughts a mix of anticipation and intrigue. In a town where subtleties ran deep and the layers of power weren't always apparent at first glance, she was beginning to realize that forging alliances and gathering insights beyond the obvious could be just as crucial to her success as solving the mysteries that Raven's Hollow held.

CHAPTER

FIVE

IN THE CRAMPED briefing room, the hum of anticipation filled the air as Sarah Morgan approached the head table, where a small tabletop podium awaited her. She looked out onto the faces of her assembled officers, their expressions a mix of curiosity and exhaustion. Next to her, several boxes of pizza sat alongside a tray of soda bottles, paper plates, and neatly folded napkins. The room was infused with the tantalizing aroma of pizza, a temporary reprieve from the weight of their responsibilities.

She recognized Sandy, the friendly face who had guided her on her first day, and Officer Paul Kneale, a seasoned officer who called her out for the dead body call. The chatter in the room gradually quieted as Sarah stepped up to the podium, her presence commanding attention.

"Alright, everyone," Sarah began, her voice projecting a blend of authority and approachability. "First of all, thank you for being here. I know it's been a challenging time, and I appreciate your dedication to Raven's Hollow Police Department. I also understand that Officer Kneale would much rather be home in bed after a very long night." A ripple of chuckles and knowing smiles spread through the room, the camaraderie of shared experiences.

She continued, "I've been briefed about the current state of affairs here, by a few of you. We're a small team, and I understand the challenges you've been facing. When I was working to complete my Ph.D. in Social Psychology, I always enjoyed meeting my new professors who took the time to introduce themselves. It gave me a handle on their personality and what they expected of me, and I plan to do the same.

"But first, let's turn to something more important," she announced, her eyes twinkling with a spark of warmth. "Please, come up and help yourself to some pizza and soda." With that invitation, a chorus of greetings, whistles, and shuffling feet filled the small room. The officers eagerly approached the spread, their weariness momentarily forgotten in the presence of food and shared camaraderie.

As they gathered around the food, Sarah observed the interactions, the way they shared jokes and stories. It was a small, meaningful step towards building rapport and trust. She knew that strong relationships within the team would be crucial for the challenges that lay ahead.

With the room abuzz in a comfortable atmosphere, Sarah's mind was already transitioning to the business at hand. She had a feeling that these officers held valuable insights about the town's mysteries, insights that would become vital as they worked to uncover the truth behind the strange occurrences. She slid a slice of pizza onto her plate and gestured for the others to do the same.

As they ate, a tentative camaraderie seemed to form. Laughter broke through, and stories were shared— brief moments of respite from the ever-present weight of the job. Sarah observed them, recognizing that this unity would be essential in the times to come.

As the initial tension began to dissipate, Sarah reached for a napkin and wiped her hands, a quiet signal that the time for casual conversation had passed. She turned her attention back to the group, her posture poised and attentive. "Alright, let's talk business," she announced, her tone shifting to one of focused determination. "Before becoming your new Chief, I was a homicide investigator with the Los Angeles Police Department." A murmur of impressed reactions rippled through the crowd, punctuated by a spontaneous "wow."

Her gaze swept across the room, locking onto each face. "We've got a unique situation on our hands, and it's going to take all of us working together to solve it," she emphasized, her words carrying a weight of shared responsibility. "And I'm not just talking about a much-earned pay raise." A chorus of hoops, hollers, and applause reverberated in the small room, the energy palpable as the officers voiced their appreciation and agreement.

The camaraderie in the room continued to grow stronger, a sense of purpose intertwining with the mutual respect they held for their new leader. Sarah understood that building a cohesive team required not just professional collaboration, but also a genuine connection among the members. With every word and gesture, she was forging those connections, cementing the foundation for what was to come.

"First and foremost, let me make it crystal clear—I will never ask you to work overtime without proper compensation. I'm committed to ensuring that every minute of your time is valued and paid for. I'll be having a direct conversation with the mayor, making sure that the labor laws of the federal government are not just words on paper." The room echoed with more cheers of approval, the officers finding reassurance in her words.

"Secondly," Sarah continued, her gaze steady and resolute, "we need to address the issue of manpower and establish a clear ranking system. In the foreseeable future, I envision having a sergeant on each shift, as well as a lieutenant who can step in when I'm not around." Amongst the nods and attentive faces, Sarah caught snippets of conversation. Sandy's voice reached her ears, saying to Officer Mary Ellen Statton, "I told you she's going to kick ass." A warmth spread through Sarah's chest, her smile reflecting the shared sentiment.

She took a moment, letting her words settle and the enthusiasm in the room subside slightly. "This won't happen overnight. It's a gradual process. But as we earn the trust and loyalty of our citizens, their voices will reverberate through the city council and even reach the mayor's office. We have the power to shape the future of Raven's Hollow—to make it a safer, more vibrant community for everyone."

The room hung in a brief, charged silence, the weight of her words sinking in. And then, as if drawn by an invisible force, a swell of applause erupted. Sarah stood before her team, realizing that this wasn't just about addressing immediate issues; it was about igniting a spark of positive change that would transform both their department and their town.

"Now, let's shift our focus back to business," she began, a sense of authority imbuing her words. "If you haven't been informed yet, Officer Kneale and I were at the scene of a homicide early this morning on Route 81. Just recently, I received a notification from the coroner's office identifying the victim as Mrs. Vivian Thompson, aged 82. I have an address for her here in Raven's Hollow and have requested the D.A.s office to issue a subpoena so we can search her home. That will probably happen on swing shift so be prepared.

I've requested aid of the sheriff's department to temporarily set on the house until we conclude this meeting. Once that is done, one of the two swing shift personnel will take over until I arrive with the warrant.

To provide us with a firsthand account, I'd like Paul, who was the first responder, despite our shortage of officers," her voice carried a hint of wry irony, triggering a few chuckles from the assembled personnel.

Her demeanor became more intent as she leaned forward, her focus squarely on Officer Kneale, who rose to his feet. After a brief clearing of his throat, his eyes met Sarah's, a mix of seriousness and perplexity evident in his gaze.

"Yes, Chief. It was... unusual. The victim, Mrs. Thompson, was found with her spleen surgically removed. It's something I've never seen before. And her expression, Chief, it was as if she'd witnessed something deeply unsettling moments before her death."

Sarah's nod conveyed both acknowledgement and appreciation. "Thank you, Paul, for that insight. As we encounter more of these distinctive cases, anticipate being exposed to them as part of your learning curve. Now, through some preliminary research, I've learned that there might have been analogous instances in the past—unexplained deaths, peculiar incidents. Have any of you here ever encountered something resembling this?"

A contemplative hush enveloped the room. One by one, gazes turned inquisitive, eyes connected, and a few officers exchanged meaningful glances. Eventually, a young officer named Dan Stansberry found his voice. "I recall hearing whispers of something like this a while back, Chief. But it was mostly talk, rumors. There wasn't any concrete evidence."

A faint smile played on Sarah's lips. "Rumors and speculations can serve as our starting point. We must gather every scrap of information available. Tomorrow morning, I'll be attending Mrs. Thompson's autopsy. I intend to grasp the situation as comprehensively as possible. If any of you possess leads or notions, please share them openly with me."

A pregnant pause followed, allowing her words to resonate. "We're united now. Together, we'll unravel this enigma and ensure justice for Mrs. Thompson and anyone else impacted. Let's pool our knowledge, collaborate closely, and unveil the truth concealed within Raven's Hollow."

As the meeting concluded, resolute gazes were exchanged among the officers. Sarah's presence had instilled a renewed sense of determination. No longer were they merely a disparate group; they stood as a unified team, propelled by a shared purpose.

CHAPTER

SIX

RESIDING ON 475, 3rd Avenue, Judith Thompson led a solitary life. Her residence was nestled within a post-World War II subdivision, where the majority of homes had undergone several renovations. However, Thompson's house seemed to defy the norm, maintaining its original charm. Evidently, she took pleasure in tending to her garden, both in the front and the back, a fact evident from the flourishing array of plants, many of which had sprung forth from bulbs she had meticulously planted.

With a search warrant grasped firmly, Chief Sarah Morgan and Officer Dan Stansberry approached the residence. Although the front door presented a barrier, their attention was drawn to a bedroom window slightly ajar at the rear of the house. Stansberry skillfully climbed through, making his way to the front entrance and granting Sarah passage.

The interior of the home carried a distinct aged aroma – the only way Sarah could describe it to herself. Every piece of furniture bore the marks of time, though they were meticulously maintained. A neatly folded blanket adorned what appeared to be her preferred armchair, positioned across from a modern flat-screen TV that seemed to be a recent addition, likely a find from the local Walmart.

Occupying a small table to the right of her chair, Sarah noted a pair of reading glasses resting atop a large-print word search book. Upon closer inspection, it was evident that Judith's mental acuity remained intact. An aging coffee maker stood on the counter, still holding half its contents, though a layer of mold had taken residence on the surface. A bowl containing overripe bananas lay nearby. The refrigerator held only a meager assortment of items, while the freezer was crammed with frozen vegetables and pot pies. A pillbox with compartments labeled for each day of the week stood on the counter, a few compartments empty while others still held pills.

Advancing through the rooms, they discovered one bedroom transformed into Judith's craft haven. Quilts she had lovingly crafted adorned the walls, draping over a well-worn recliner in the corner. The master bedroom, dwarfed in comparison to contemporary constructions, housed an unmade bed, its foot facing a bathroom. A pair of glasses occupied the left nightstand, which was the same room Officer Stansberry had accessed through the open window.

Despite everything appearing in its place, an uneasy feeling lingered with Sarah, although she couldn't quite put her finger on it. Just as the sense of unease settled, both she and Stansberry heard a knock at the door. Officer Stansberry, dressed in his uniform, stepped forward to answer it.

"Hello, my name is Charlotte. I live next door. Is Judith alright? My husband and I haven't seen her in a few days," the concerned neighbor inquired. Sarah and Stansberry stepped out onto the porch to engage with Charlotte, an elderly African American woman, seemingly in her eighties or perhaps her early nineties.

"Have you been acquainted with Mrs. Thompson for quite a while?" Sarah inquired.

"Oh dear, it must be around seventy years or so. We both moved in around the same time, once they finished building our homes. Her husband, Clarence, passed away in 1991, and she's been a widow ever since. Is she alright? If she's in the hospital, I can keep an eye on her house," Charlotte offered with concern.

"Did Mrs. Thompson drive?" Sarah probed, noting the absence of a vehicle in the garage.

"Oh no, she gave up her license a long while ago. She was quite upset with her doctor when he told her she had to stop driving," Charlotte responded, her head shaking as if recalling those moments. "Once we older folks hit a certain age, they start giving you memory tests. Sam, my husband, and I know it well – time catches up to you. Judith would use Uber or

49

one of those taxi services, or she'd get her groceries delivered right to her doorstep. Let me tell you, both of you, Judith was as sharp as a tack. She loved playing Monopoly, and I swear, nobody could beat her."

Following the interview with Charlotte and escorting her back to her home, where they also encountered her husband Sam, who was an invalid, Sarah delivered the somber news of Judith's passing. Charlotte's frame trembled as tears flowed, her distress concealed from her husband. They gently settled her in a chair, allowing her time to regain her composure after the shock.

With no concrete information about the arrangements for Mrs. Thompson's final rites, Sarah jotted down the phone number of the coroner's office and handed it to Charlotte. Sarah resolved to remind herself to notify Chelsea about the impending call from Charlotte.

They concluded their search of Mrs. Thompson's residence, dusting for prints on the bedroom window as well as the outside and inside door handles. They assumed that most would belong to the victim, but it had to be done. It was during a walk around the perimeter of the house that they found the only tangible piece of evidence. A foot impression in the recently turned over soil outside the window that Stansberry climbed in from. It wasn't the impression of his combat boot, but inside a smooth surfaced size 11 imprint.

Stansberry meticulously photographed, cast, and then carefully lifted the footprint as Sarah looked on. With these pieces in hand, the puzzle was clear: they needed to locate a shoe that could have made such an impression and identify the individual who wore it.

Sarah awoke to find her bedsheet drenched from night sweats, her white tee-shirt clinging uncomfortably to her skin, and even her pillow dampened. Once again, the specter of her nightmare had forced her to relive the horrific memory—the killing of her husband and four-year-old daughter by Sam Wright, a serial killer who had eluded the grasp of law enforcement for more than a decade. It was Sarah who had finally tracked him down, inching closer to his capture.

As he sensed her proximity, Wright had slipped into stalking mode, biding his time until Jim, her husband, returned home one fateful evening after picking up Tamatha from their babysitter.

But the chilling depths of Wright's sadism didn't stop at the murder of her family. After executing them with cold precision, he had arranged their lifeless bodies on the living room floor, their faces turned upwards, and their hands intertwined—a grotesque tableau of his malevolence.

Sarah had harbored the intent to personally end Wright's life during his capture. Yet, the presence of a multitude of other officers had thwarted her plan, robbing the taxpayers of California of salvation from the impending spectacle of a protracted trial. A life sentence, devoid of any possibility for parole, provided scant reparation for the gaping void left by her loss.

She detested the trite sentiments parroted by talking heads and politicians—how the capture of suspects allegedly brought closure to the victims' friends and family. She saw it for what it was: utter nonsense.

Instead of finding solace, her mind remained plagued by relentless questions. What had her loved ones been doing just before the brutal attack? Had they experienced prolonged agony, or had the ordeal been a swift end, irrespective of what the coroner's reports might conventionally state?

In a bid to numb her sorrow, she had sought solace in alcohol. However, she soon recognized the treacherous path it could pave, potentially putting her job—the cornerstone of her existence—in jeopardy. With the stark reality in mind, she redirected her efforts toward a healthier outlet: rigorous training in Shotokan Karate. Through unwavering dedication, she attained her black belt, her instructor marveling at the swiftness of her achievement, hailing it as an accomplishment that came close to setting a record.

Sarah removed all of her bedding and place it in the dryer. She was to meet a real estate agent that evening to check on a few houses that she liked based so far on a Zillow search. With the real estate market in a down turn, she felt now was the time to invest in a purchase.

After a brisk shower, a bowl of cereal, and two cups of coffee, she hurried out the door, her mind already contemplating the tasks ahead beyond the visit to the coroner's office.

"Morning, Chief," greeted Sandy cheerfully as Sarah stepped into the office. "Dr. Lawrence sent the details regarding the victim's identity. I've placed them on your desk."

"Thanks, Sandy. Any chance the coffee's brewing?" Sarah asked, reminiscing that she'd stashed her coffee cup in her briefcase the night before – a detail she now retrieved.

"Absolutely. The bakery down the street dropped off a dozen donuts as a welcoming gesture. They mentioned you're welcome to swing by when you've got a moment."

"Well, that's thoughtful of them. Let's set them out so the night shift can enjoy them, and make sure Mary Ellen gets her share when she arrives. No calls last night, so I'm guessing it was a peaceful evening?" she inquired.

"Absolutely quiet. You've got a slot at the coroner's office at 10 AM, and you'd asked me to compile all the files on the missing person reports. I've placed them on your desk as well."

"Looks like you're the epitome of organization," Sarah remarked, pouring coffee into her cup and snagging a donut before making her way to her office.

Taking hold of the uppermost file from the stack of missing persons reports, she opened it. The photograph depicted Marie Kelly, a 21-year-old white female. Quite charming, Sarah noted. According to the file, Marie had been reported missing by her mother, who indicated that she hadn't returned from her junior college as usual, and her friends were also unable to get in touch with her. Calls went straight to voicemail. As she finished perusing the file, Sarah discovered a rudimentary missing person report, suggesting that there hadn't been an extensive effort at that time to locate her.

Proceeding to the second file, mindful of the ticking clock, she delved in. Naomi George, an African woman of 52 years, displayed an infectious smile in her photograph affixed to the document's upper left corner. Her figure carried some extra weight, noticeable even from the photo. The report had been filed by her husband, Willie, who had been married to her for over two decades. Strangely, the report seemed to emphasize more the toll Naomi's vanishing had exacted on Willie, rather than providing pertinent details about her daily life. Once again, the report was found lacking in substantial documentation.

She took a break from reviewing the files and after getting a warmup cup of coffee, went out to visit with Sandy. "I've been wondering, where are the officer's training files and background checks stored?" she inquired.

Sandy quickly replied, "All of that information is kept in the HR department, right next to the mayor's office. Is there something specific you're looking for?"

"No, not particularly. I just thought it would be good to familiarize myself more with my staff. Thanks. I might swing by later to take a look, once I'm done with the autopsy. You know you can reach me on my cell if you need anything." With that, Sarah made her way to the last remaining patrol car and headed towards the coroner's office. Arriving a full ten minutes ahead of schedule, she considered that Dr. Lawrence might appreciate her punctuality.

"Chief, your early arrival is quite commendable. I appreciate that. Your protective gear has been neatly arranged for you right over there. Fortunately, we seem to share similar height and weight, so the fit should be appropriate," she informed. A small container of Vick's ointment was extended as an offer, yet Sarah revealed her own. "Clearly, you've been through this before," Dr. Lawrence remarked with a hint of admiration.

A young woman entered the room, walking in from a smaller adjacent office while carrying a notebook. "Chief, allow me to introduce Jenna, my assistant. She was absent on the morning we discovered the unfortunate situation with Mrs. Thompson here," Dr. Lawrence introduced. Following this, Lawrence activated the sizable, circular operating lamp positioned above the body. "Alright, let's commence."

Sarah observed attentively as Dr. Lawrence carried out a standard autopsy, but her focus was particularly fixed on the back and spine region of the deceased. "I can now affirm my initial observation at the scene –

the victim's spleen had been surgically removed, and there's minimal evidence of trauma in the surrounding area. The instrument employed appeared to be of surgical grade. There are no indications of hesitancy in the actions," Dr. Lawrence concluded.

As she started to peel off her gloves, she delivered one last comment into the microphone suspended from the surgical lamp. "The primary factor contributing to the demise of this individual was a myocardial infarction. Judging by the tension in the facial muscles, it suggests that the victim experienced a profoundly fearful state prior to death. The removal of the spleen occurred post-mortem."

CHAPTER

SEVEN

C HIEF SARAH MORGAN reclined in
her chair, her thoughts consumed by the
disturbing images she had witnessed during
the autopsy. The elderly woman's death had etched an
unsettling imprint on her mind, and the inexplicable
removal of the woman's spleen added an additional
layer of intrigue to the perplexing case.

The restaurant they were in had been fashioned
from a quaint house, its living room now transformed
into a dining space. Fifteen tables, draped in crisp
white tablecloths and adorned with arranged settings,
filled the room. As a waiter meticulously filled their
water glasses and presented menus, Sarah found herself
across from Dr. Chelsea Lawrence, the town's coroner,
who had insisted on being called Chelsea. Amidst the
gentle clinking of cutlery and hushed conversations,
Sarah couldn't shake the growing sense that something
much larger and more ominous loomed behind the
recent events.

Absently stirring her coffee, Sarah eventually broke the silence. "Chelsea, there's something more to these cases than meets the eye. The pattern you described, the extreme fear exhibited by the victims coupled with the removal of their spleens in a method suggesting medical expertise... it's all too calculated."

Chelsea sighed, her gaze fixed on the bowl of soup before her. "Sarah, I've spent over a decade as the coroner in this town, and I've never encountered anything of this nature. The spleen removal alone is perplexing, almost ritualistic. I even entertained the possibility of a cult, but given Raven's Hallow's limited resources and the mayor's priorities, it's hard to imagine."

Sarah's mind raced, connecting the dots. "And these victims, different ages, backgrounds, walks of life... the common thread being their cause of death: extreme fear." A shiver ran down Sarah's spine as the implications began to settle. "Someone is exploiting their fears, weaponizing them for some sinister purpose."

Leaning forward, Chelsea's voice dropped to a hushed tone. "There's something else you should know. Some locals have started murmuring about an old legend—the 'Fearmonger.' A malevolent spirit that thrives on fear and exacts vengeance on those it judges guilty."

Sarah raised an eyebrow, intrigued despite her skepticism. "A vengeful spirit? Chelsea, we're dealing with tangible problems here, not folklore."

Chelsea nodded, acknowledging the point. "I understand, but sometimes, myths can contain a kernel of truth. However, what we're facing is human in origin, make no mistake. Someone with knowledge of anatomy and a twisted sense of retribution."

The puzzle pieces clicked into place in Sarah's mind. "So, we have an antagonist, orchestrating these deaths to unfold like a macabre punishment."

Chelsea's expression grew solemn. "Given the evidence, that's the most plausible explanation. Whoever it is, they're manipulating fear, turning it into a lethal weapon."

Sarah's determination hardened as she contemplated the gravity of their task. "Then we have to confront this head-on. I need to delve deeper into these cases, find the connections, uncover the motives behind this dark scheme."

"Sarah, can I ask you something personal?" Chelsea's voice held a note of sensitivity.

"Of course, Chelsea," Sarah replied. "You're probably one of the few people in this town I feel completely at ease with. Well, there's Amanda, the mayor's secretary; she seems nice. And I can't forget Sandy, my desk officer. So, feel free to ask away."

"When we first met, I could see the weariness in your eyes. I mean, we were all tired back then, waking up at ungodly hours to reach crime scenes. But even now, in this restaurant, you still seem fatigued. Are you having trouble sleeping?"

Sarah decided to open up a bit, knowing that Chelsea's background as a medical doctor might offer some understanding, even though she believed her issues were more psychological than medical. Suppressing the urge to cry, she began to share her story with Chelsea, recounting the painful memory of her husband and 4-year-old daughter falling victim to a serial killer.

Chelsea's expression shifted to one of shock and empathy. "Oh my God, Sarah. I can't even begin to express how sorry I am. Have they managed to catch the person responsible?"

"Yes, we caught him, and he's been sentenced to life without parole," Sarah replied with a hint of resolution.

Chelsea's voice took on a more vehement tone. "Sounds like the asshole got off too easy, if you ask me. Excuse the language."

Sarah nodded, understanding the sentiment. "It wasn't my first choice either. These days, I'm tossing and turning all night, and I sometimes wake up drenched in sweat."

Reaching into her purse, Chelsea retrieved a small plastic baggie and a vial of pills. "These are 10 mg Valium tablets." She counted out eight and placed them in the baggie. "I want you to take one as soon as you're safely home before dinner. It won't be long before it takes effect and grants you a peaceful sleep. I realize I forgot to give you my business card. It has my personal cell number on it. Don't hesitate to call me anytime."

Sarah accepted the Valium with gratitude, then took out a small spiral notepad. "Thank you, Chelsea. Apologies, I don't have business cards yet." She jotted down her cell number on a piece of the notepad and passed it to Chelsea.

As their lunch concluded, the chief and the coroner were united by the realization that their journey for answers had just begun. The sinister orchestrator behind these deaths would soon learn that they were facing a force of justice as unyielding as the fear they sought to exploit.

Leaving the restaurant behind, Sarah made her way to the Human Resources department, conveniently housed within the same building as Mayor Wadsworth's office. With a stroke of luck, she hoped to avoid any encounters with him. Approaching the counter, Sarah introduced herself as the freshly appointed police chief. The receptionist's demeanor quickly shifted from welcoming to guarded, hinting at an undercurrent of bureaucracy. Undeterred, Sarah pressed on, her tone firm as she requested access to the background investigation and training records of her staff. The receptionist's features hardened, her questions slicing through the air with a hint of skepticism.

"Chief, I'm not sure. The files are typically locked away, and it's usually only the Mayor who's granted access to them," the receptionist offered hesitantly.

Sarah let out a thoughtful hum. "Isn't it peculiar, though? The Chief of Police doesn't have access to records detailing the backgrounds of my own officers or any gaps in their training. Frankly, it's a glaring inconsistency. If I were an attorney, I'd have a field day if one of our officers were to cause harm or, heaven forbid, injure someone. I can envision settlements reaching well into the two to three million range."

"Hi, Sarah," Amanda greeted with a radiant smile as she approached the counter where Sarah was waiting. "Is there something I can assist you with?"

Before Sarah could respond, the clerk briefed Amanda on her request to access the background and training records of her officers. "Absolutely, that's a reasonable request," Amanda replied without skipping a beat. She turned to Sarah, her expression encouraging. "Sarah, let's get this sorted. Sally here will guide us to where the files are kept. There's even a desk and a lamp nearby where you can set up comfortably."

Sally, pleased to have the mayor's secretary's approval, nodded and quickly arranged clearance for them to access the files. With enthusiasm, she led the way to the designated area, making sure to offer Sarah a cup of coffee and an open-ended offer of assistance if needed.

With a parting nod from Sally, Amanda shot Sarah a playful wink. "Give me a heads-up if you encounter any more gatekeepers." With that, she pivoted gracefully and maneuvered her way through the labyrinth of desks, navigating the office's bustling activity. Her destination: the main hallway leading to the mayor's office.

Several hours and three cups of coffee were expended before Sarah completed her exhaustive perusal of her officers' personnel and training records. There were no groundbreaking revelations unearthed in their backgrounds.

Among her team, Carl Thompson, her flex officer, carried the experience of two tours in Afghanistan, a testament to his military background. Dan Stansberry, on the other hand, had fulfilled a tour of duty in Iraq, his service record denoting his commitment to duty.

Meanwhile, Mary Ellen's profile initially displayed aspirations towards a nursing degree, but circumstances led her to change course and embrace her current role. I wonder why? Sarah thought.

Officer Kneale, a Raven's Hallow native, appeared to be a product of local recruitment efforts, raised within the very fabric of the town. Sarah marked him as someone to interview, particularly regarding the local murmurs of the 'Fearmonger.'

In another intriguing turn, Tim Moore, a swing-shift officer, held a BA in forestry, though his academic journey revealed a notable number of Criminal Justice courses. Sarah made a mental note to delve into Moore's background further, curious about the transition from forestry to law enforcement.

Yet, it was their training records that elicited a genuine shock from Sarah. The entries revealed a mere scrape of the essentials required for an officer's induction. The realization struck her with disconcerting force. Later investigation would confirm her suspicion: the mayor's firm grip on the police department's budget was stifling her officers' access to advanced training. Sarah knew that once she established herself firmly in her role, she and the honorable mayor would inevitably find themselves locking horns. She thanked Sally on her way out telling her that the files were ready to be secured.

CHAPTER

EIGHT

THE TUDOR-STYLE RESIDENCE and its surrounding grounds exuded an aura of affluence. The meticulously groomed lawn and artfully crafted Japanese gardens evoked the ambiance of exclusive country clubs or secluded private retreats. A sweeping resin-bound driveway, its graceful curve encompassing the expanse, led to an opulent spectacle—an expansive, multi-tiered fountain featuring a mermaid cradling a seashell. Water cascaded from the shell's embrace, forming elegant arcs that splashed into a serene retaining pond, where lilies blossomed in vibrant profusion.

Upon crossing the imposing threshold, one entered a realm adorned with marbled flooring, an expansive canvas of opulence. The grand staircase, an architectural marvel in itself, reached its zenith before gracefully branching in opposing directions, a symphony of curves leading to various chambers. To the right of the staircase's foot, an entrance beckoned—a vast library, its ambiance enhanced by polished mahogany bookshelves cradling a wealth of leather-bound volumes.

Adjacent to this literary haven lay a gourmet-style kitchen, where pots dangled from above, poised over a sprawling expanse of granite counter. Yet, hidden from casual view, a deliberate observer would discern a concealed doorway adjacent to the library's entrance. This discreet portal, when coaxed open, revealed a secret: a spiral staircase winding down into the basement depths.

The air was saturated with the acrid scent of formaldehyde, a potent and pungent fragrance that intermingled notes of vinegar and scorched matches, enveloping the room. The epicenter of this olfactory assault was a capacious and meticulously equipped laboratory. Here, an array of large glass vessels stood as custodians to creatures in varying stages of development, reminiscent of colossal centipedes frozen in time, their eerie forms on display.

Dr. Adrian Sinclair, a distinguished neuroscientist of renown, was deeply immersed in his task—meticulously dissecting one of the enigmatic creatures. Draped in a pristine white lab coat and sporting a set of orascoptic loupe headgear, he toiled with intense focus. The dulcet strains of Mozart's composition lingered softly in the background, creating an ethereal backdrop to his painstaking exploration.

Standing tall at a commanding 6 feet 2 inches, Dr. Sinclair cut an imposing figure. His dark hair was slicked back, harmonizing with his slender mustache. His concentration was shattered by an abrupt noise, prompting him to pivot. With determined strides, he advanced toward a substantial cage, within which a creature akin to the one under his dissection was in motion. Its' much larger form lifted, its immense mandibles probing the air as it sought a route of escape.

"Calm down, Medusa. It's not yet time for your feeding. How about a small indulgence, just so I can take your measurements?" With a firm grip on a substantial turkey baster syringe, he carefully opened a generously sized glass container. It held a concoction that emanated an overpowering odor – a mixture of human blood and minute insect fragments suspended in a mostly liquid solution.

Once the baster had been filled to its capacity, he cautiously lowered it into the cage, expertly navigating the bars. With a skillful press of the plunger, he injected the mixture into a waiting bowl positioned in the cage's left corner.

Observing Medusa's reaction, Sinclair witnessed her swift crawl to the bowl, where she began to consume the provisions with an almost eager appetite. Meanwhile, he continued to empty the contents of the baster, ensuring every last drop was delivered. Swiftly retrieving a cloth measuring tape, he positioned himself at the opposite end of the cage, conducting a meticulous assessment of the creature's growth.

"Incredible," he remarked with a mixture of fascination and scientific appreciation. "Two inches of growth in just five days. My growth hormone is working." Resuming his place at the worktable, Sinclair directed his attention to the dissected remains of the creature. His hands deftly recorded his observations in the pages of his lab notebook, all the while a soft hum escaped his lips, harmonizing with a delicate Mozart melody that danced through the air.

The following morning greeted Sarah with a sense of complete rejuvenation. The Valium had undoubtedly performed its intended magic, she mused. Engaging in a series of gentle stretching exercises, she felt her muscles awaken before proceeding to take a refreshing shower and select her attire for the day. Although the bed-and-breakfast where she currently resided offered a continental breakfast, Sarah's appetite craved a heartier option.

Guiding her car through the streets, she arrived at a charming diner that proudly boasted the town's finest pancakes, a claim she intended to put to the test. Seated promptly, she perused the extensive double-sided menu and settled on a satisfying combination: a stack of pancakes, a generous serving of hash browns, accompanied by flavorful link sausages, all complemented by a steady flow of coffee.

While her breakfast was being prepared, she glanced at her phone and realized she had slept through a call from her realtor, Cindy. The memory of her late-night venture, submitting an offer for a 3-bedroom, 2-bath house not far from the heart of the town, came flooding back. An undercurrent of excitement mingled with her surprise as she listened to Cindy's voicemail, confirming that her offer had been accepted.

With the early hour displaying only 6:45 on her phone, Sarah made a mental note to reach out to Cindy after 9, allowing for a more reasonable time to discuss the intricacies of the upcoming process. She needed to confirm if the seller had indeed agreed to her request for a 21-day escrow, a critical detail in the journey towards her new home.

Savoring what she deemed her final cup of coffee, she retrieved her spiral notebook and initiated her task list. Topping the roster was a resolute notation to contact Cindy. Sequentially, she penned an entry for Sandy, delegating the responsibility of compiling an inventory of advanced officer courses alongside their corresponding class schedules.

This strategic initiative aimed to facilitate the process of enhancing her team's training. Admittedly, this decision might entail her temporarily covering those shifts, potentially single-handedly, a necessary compromise as she persevered until securing additional resources from the mayor's office.

She jotted down a reminder to share a cup of coffee with Officer Paul Kneale. Given his roots in Raven's Hallow, he likely possessed insights into the Fearmonger legend. Chelsea's words echoed in her mind: 'sometimes, myths can hold fragments of reality.'

Among her tasks, she aimed to review her department's budget. Amanda, the mayor's secretary, might be able to discreetly provide this information without the mayor's awareness. Sarah acknowledged that an eventual clash between her and Wadsworth was inevitable. Equipping herself with a comprehensive understanding of the data beforehand would enable her to counter any potential excuses he might conjure up.

The subsequent entry was marked with an asterisk, indicating its significance. She recorded her intention to make an anonymous call to the Department of Labor, drawing attention to the conditions of officers within the Raven's Hallow Police Department. A hint of a smile tugged at her lips as she pondered the mayor's response to the scrutiny of his stance on overtime pay.

The last item on her list was a reminder to persist with her examination of missing person reports. Additionally, she aimed to dispatch inquiries to neighboring jurisdictions, encompassing instances of body dumps. "Seems like a packed day ahead," she mused, taking a final sip of her dwindling coffee.

As the morning light filtered through the windows of Dr. Sinclair's dimly lit laboratory, he meticulously examined his notes and observations from the recent Tingler experiment. The room was filled with an air of anticipation, the hum of the air conditioning unit serving as a constant backdrop to his thoughts.

A faint vibration disrupted his concentration, emanating from his phone resting on the corner of the cluttered worktable. He retrieved the device, its screen illuminating his focused expression. A text message notification blinked at him, and he tapped the screen to reveal the message.

The sender's name was known to him, but the message itself held an enigmatic quality. "Have you found a suitable candidate for the next contribution to our research?" the text inquired. The words seemed innocuous, yet an undercurrent of intrigue surrounded them.

Sinclair's eyes lingered on the message, his thoughts weaving through a labyrinth of possibilities. The identity of the sender was a secret shared only between them, a connection rooted in their shared pursuits. He contemplated the implications of this inquiry, his mind racing with the intricate web of motivations and intentions that intertwined their fates.

Closing the message, he leaned back in his chair, his fingers tapping rhythmically against the worn armrest. The day's experiments and revelations were momentarily overshadowed by the cryptic communication. He was no stranger to the complexities of their arrangement, the alliance that promised advancement in their shared pursuits.

Sinclair's gaze drifted toward the cage that housed the evolving tingler specimen. The creature's movements were a testament to his dedication, a living embodiment of his experiments' progress. Yet, beyond the confines of the laboratory, a world of secrecy and intrigue awaited him.

In the depths of his mind, he contemplated his response to the text. A decision loomed before him, a choice that would further entwine his fate with that of his mysterious counterpart. The weight of their collaboration was palpable, a dance between shadow and ambition that drove them forward, no matter the consequences.

Letting out a composed sigh, Sinclair's focus returned to his meticulous notes, although the weight of the text message hung in the air like an unanswered riddle. The laboratory reverberated once more with the familiar sounds of pens scratching paper, the subtle hum of equipment, and the rhythmic pulse of a scientist's heart. In this sanctuary of exploration, his existence remained interwoven with the puzzle that had suddenly reappeared in his life.

His fingers danced across the keyboard of his computer, crafting a response that held an air of finality. "Tonight," he typed, a simple word that resonated with anticipation. The enigma that had enveloped him, the collaboration that blurred the line between purpose and secrecy, was once again set in motion. As the message was sent, Sinclair sensed a shift in the currents of his reality, a reminder that the worlds of science and intrigue were forever entangled.

CHAPTER

NINE

S ARAH WELCOMED SANDY as she arrived, impressively beating the front desk officer of the day shift by a solid 20 minutes. "I brought blueberry muffins," Sarah mentioned with a warm smile. "I stopped at the bakery on my way here, and they just seemed too tempting to resist."

Sandy's response was a beaming smile. "Chief, that's really thoughtful of you. Let me brew a fresh pot of coffee so we can get to these muffins together." Sarah strolled alongside Sandy, curious to observe the coffee supplies' location and Sandy's coffee-making process – knowledge that could prove valuable for moments when Sandy might be absent due to illness or training.

"You sure got here early," Sandy said. "I think our old chief only beat me here on those days that he had to cover the graveyard shift. You must be full of energy today."

"Actually, it is more out of joy since I learned over breakfast that my offer on a home was accepted by the seller. In 21-days, I hope to move in."

"Gee, that is exciting. I hope to have enough money someday to at least buy a condo. I can't offer a home here in Raven's Hollow. Where is it at?"

"It is a 3-bedroom, 2-bath home on Hickory Street, mid-block."

"Oh, those are all real nice homes over there and it is always quiet. We never get a call for service there unless it is a medical emergency. Well, congratulations."

"Thanks," Sarah responded, both of them observing the coffee maker diligently at work. "Sandy, when you have a moment, I'd like you to look into how we can access a comprehensive list of advanced officer training courses from the state. Details like course descriptions, dates, times, and locations. It's about time we take our team's training to the next level."

Sandy's face lit up with understanding. "I know exactly where to find that information. But, can I ask you a question?"

"Of course. I'm guessing you're wondering how I plan to handle the overtime issue while sending everyone for training," Sarah answered, a slight grin forming.

Sandy nodded, letting the question hang unspoken. "Leave that to me," Sarah reassured with a confident smile, adding a touch of substitute sugar and creamer to her coffee cup. The entrance bell rang announcing either the arrival of Mary Ellen or Paul Kneale. It turned out to be both arriving at the same time.

"Hey, everyone. The Chief brought some blueberry muffins," Sarah announced, the warmth of camaraderie evident in her tone.

"Fantastic," Mary Ellen exclaimed, her path swiftly leading her to the coffee pot. "I overslept this morning, missed breakfast. Thanks a lot, Chief."

Kneale chimed in, reaching for a muffin as he spoke, "Yes, Chief, thanks for this."

As Mary Ellen returned the coffee pot, Kneale moved in to pour his coffee. "Paul, once you're settled, can I steal a few minutes of your time before you head off to bed? I want to discuss something I learned from Dr. Lawrence."

"Sure thing. Let me just stow my things in my locker," he replied, swiftly departing and soon returning, coffee mug in hand. With a nod towards his colleagues, he made his way into Sarah's office, leaving the hallway bustling with the aroma of coffee and the promise of the conversation ahead.

Paul leaned back slightly in his chair, a casual smile playing on his lips. "Oh, the Fearmonger, huh? That's just one of those local tales, Chief. You know how it goes – small towns tend to brew up some wild stories to keep things interesting."

Sarah nodded, acknowledging his response. She was well aware of how such legends often sprouted from the fertile soil of imagination, feeding off the community's collective fears and uncertainties. However, she remained resolute, not ready to let the topic slide just yet.

"Absolutely, Paul. I get that," she replied, her tone even and professional. "But sometimes, these myths have a way of lingering for a reason. People don't just make them up out of thin air."

Paul chuckled softly, his expression one of gentle skepticism. "Sure, Chief. It's all good fun. But trust me, there's no creature lurking around here, spooking folks to death."

Sarah maintained her composure, her eyes locked onto Paul's. "I appreciate your perspective, Paul. But indulge me for a moment. It's not about believing in these stories; it's about understanding them. Sometimes, myths carry fragments of truth hidden beneath layers of exaggeration."

Paul's resistance began to waver, sensing that Sarah wasn't about to let go of the topic easily. He sighed, realizing that he might as well share a bit more information. "Alright, Chief. There might be some folks around here who still swear they've seen something, especially in the woods. But it's just imagination playing tricks on them."

Sarah's interest was piqued. While Paul's explanation still fit within the realm of superstition, she sensed there might be more to the legend than he was revealing. "Thanks, Paul. I know it might sound like I'm chasing ghosts here, but sometimes these stories have roots worth investigating."

Paul nodded, a slight grin forming on his face. "You know, Chief, since we are talking about ghosts, spirits and stuff, back in '59, they claimed a giant centipede attacked a woman at the silent movie theater. Called it the 'Silent Terror.' But nothing ever came of it, as far as I know."

Sarah raised an eyebrow. "A giant centipede attacking a moviegoer? That sounds like quite the tale."

Paul laughed, the skepticism returning to his tone. "Yeah, exactly. A lot of fuss back then, but it turned out to be just a bunch of exaggerated rumors. You know how stories like that tend to grow over time."

Sarah smiled, appreciating his candor. "You might be right, Paul. But I've learned that sometimes, beneath the exaggerations, there's a seed of truth waiting to be uncovered."

Paul shook his head playfully. "Well, Chief, if we end up chasing centipedes, I hope we've got some big boots."

They shared a chuckle, the conversation blending a touch of levity with the mysteries that Raven's Hallow held. In that moment, Sarah knew that even if the Fearmonger legend was nothing more than a tale, the town's history was rich with stories waiting to be unraveled.

Once Paul had departed, Sarah glanced at her watch. The time was nearing 8:30, prompting her to dial Amanda's number. As the call connected, she was greeted with the official announcement from Amanda that she had reached the mayor's office.

"Good morning, Amanda. This is Chief Morgan, or rather, Sarah. I hope your day is off to a good start so far."

"It certainly is, though it's still quite early. How about you, Sarah? Are you settling into the job well?"

"I am, thank you. I've got a fantastic staff here. The reason I'm reaching out is to discuss the budget for my department. It's another detail that seemed to have slipped through during the transition. Would it be feasible to obtain access to it? If this request puts you in an uncomfortable position with the mayor, please feel free to consider this conversation non-existent."

Amanda chuckled. "Sarah, your budget details didn't simply fall through the cracks. When it comes to matters like that, the mayor keeps things quite close to the vest. I don't recall him being upfront about the budget with your predecessor either.

Here's an idea. The mayor will be out for most of today, rubbing elbows with the Dreamscape executives at their upcoming location. They've invited him to lunch so I don't expect him back until later this afternoon if ever.

How about this? I'll secure a copy of your budget, and if your schedule permits, we could grab lunch. If you're a fan of a juicy burger and fries, there's a fantastic spot just two blocks away. Come on by my office around 11:30, and I can give us a lift out there."

Things were gradually falling into place, Sarah mused. Her cellphone chimed, revealing an incoming

78

call from Cindy, her realtor. She realized she had forgotten to reach out earlier that morning. "Cindy, I'm truly sorry for not calling you earlier today. I only saw your text at 6 AM. I'm absolutely thrilled that my offer was accepted."

"Well, Sarah, I've got even more positive news for you. Not only did they accept your offer and agree to a 21-day escrow, but they're also wondering if you'd be interested in a day-to-day rental arrangement until the deed transfer is complete. Since the house is vacant and your credit is excellent, they're quite confident you'll sail through the escrow process."

"Oh my God, that's fantastic! Please convey to them that I'm absolutely interested. If you can manage to get the necessary paperwork ready, I can drop by later today and sign it."

No worries about coming in. I'll have the documents sent your way via DocuSign, and you should be all set. I'll adjust the loan agreement to include the day-to-day rental arrangement. This way, everything will come together through escrow. Keep an eye out for the documents needing your signature."

CHAPTER

TEN

D R. SINCLAIR'S LABORATORY was a sanctuary of shadows and the hum of machinery. Dim light cast eerie shadows across the walls, creating an atmosphere of otherworldly secrecy. At the center of the room, a large triple thick plexiglass cage housed the growing tingler, Medussa. The creature's once diminutive form had expanded exponentially, stretching nearly five feet in length. Its segmented body pulsed with an unnatural vitality, a testament to Sinclair's relentless experimentation. It had twice been able to stretch the stainless-steel bars that held it.

Sinclair stood before the cage; his eyes fixed on Medussa's sinuous movements. The tingler's every twitch and contortion held him captivated, a macabre ballet of scientific curiosity. His hands, once steady and precise, trembled with excitement as he observed the tingler's evolution. The tingler, in turn, responded to his presence, its sensory antennae probing the air as if seeking its creator's acknowledgment.

The tingler's movements became increasingly pronounced, its antenna-like appendages twitching with an almost sentient purpose. Sinclair's fingers brushed against the cage, his detachment from ethical boundaries now complete. He whispered to the creature as if it could comprehend his words, a mad scientist addressing his creation with reverence.

In the midst of his growing detachment, Sinclair's obsession grew ever more consuming. The tingler was no longer just a scientific curiosity; it was a manifestation of his ambition, an embodiment of his unraveling sense of morality. As the tingler continued to evolve, so did Sinclair's own transformation, forging a path toward discovery that was both exhilarating and perilous.

Draped in attire reminiscent of a ninja, Dr. Sinclair concealed himself in the shadows, his form obscured by the folds of dark fabric. Black gloves adorned his hands, a stark contrast to the meticulous white coat he had once worn with pride. The transformation was complete, a reflection of his descent into the shadows of his own creation.

His medical bath contained the vessel of his sinister intent; a vial of chloroform. The liquid held the promise of unconsciousness, a tool he wielded with cold detachment. With deliberate precision, Sinclair stepped through the laboratory, his steps hushed by the weight of his dark purpose.

Sinclair's vehicle awaited him like a loyal accomplice, its engine humming in the stillness of the night. He slid into the driver's seat, a man consumed by obsession, driven to cross lines that he had once sworn never to breach. His eyes held an unsettling determination, focused solely on the task that lay ahead.

The house, a distant beacon in the night, had been meticulously scouted. Sinclair's obsession had guided his steps, leaving no room for uncertainty. He knew his target, their routines, and their vulnerabilities. Every detail had been calculated, every potential obstacle weighed and considered.

As he navigated the darkened streets, Sinclair's mind raced with a mixture of anticipation and trepidation. The tingler's growth had become inextricably linked to his own transformation. The boundaries that had once defined him had blurred, reshaped by the very thing he had created.

Arriving at the target's residence, Sinclair's pulse quickened. This was the culmination of his experiments, the embodiment of his obsession. He was no longer a scientist but a puppeteer, orchestrating a macabre symphony with lives hanging in the balance.

With silent steps, Sinclair approached the house, his ninja-like garb allowing him to blend seamlessly into the shadows. His gloved fingers wrapped around the vial of chloroform, a chilling reminder of his new identity. His heart pounded in his chest, a mix of adrenaline and a growing detachment from the ethical boundaries that had once constrained him.

As the night air hung heavy with the weight of his actions, Dr. Sinclair took a deep breath. The tingler's growth had unlocked something primal within him, a darkness that had always existed but had been suppressed by societal norms. He was now a creature of the night, driven by his obsession to pursue the boundaries of science and morality, heedless of the consequences that lay ahead.

The teenager, her identity fading into obscurity, claimed the rear bedroom—a sanctuary of seclusion, set apart from her parents' realm. Serendipitously, he found her window slightly open, a nod to the enduring warmth that embraced the night. The moon's soft radiance provided ample light to sketch the layout of her room, tracing the silhouette of her slumbering figure on the bed. As she was deaf and mute, he harbored no worries about the slight sounds he might create while entering through her bedroom window.

During his investigation, he discovered that Dr. Warren Chapin had made unsuccessful attempts to utilize LSD as a means of inducing fear within himself. He frequently contemplated the possible reaction of a person's tingler in the scenario of their muteness, pondering how, unable to scream, the host's escalating fear might cause the tingler to expand to a fatal extent, ultimately rupturing the spleen and leading to death.

Hence, the choice fell upon this adolescent. A plethora of queries could find their answers. What dimensions does a person's tingler assume from infancy to eighteen? How great a dosage of fear would be imperative to prompt the tingler to claim a life so youthful? The sole unpredictable element remains his awareness of any prevailing conditions that might influence the experiment's result. Nevertheless, he mused, alternative candidates are perpetually within reach.

He strategically parked his vehicle near the residence, careful not to arouse any suspicions. His hand brushed against the front pocket of his jacket, reassuring himself of the vial of chloroform and the cloth, both ready for the impending moment. With his readiness confirmed, he gingerly raised the window just enough for a seamless entry into the room.

Standing beside her, he tuned in to the rhythm of her breath, a sign that she was in the depths of slumber. Retrieving the vial and cloth, he allowed the contents to flow generously onto the fabric while averting his face to minimize inhalation of the fumes. Contrary to the misconception perpetuated by movies, many in society believe chloroform's effects to be immediate. However, in reality, it takes several minutes for the compound to induce unconsciousness in a person.

As predicted, she succumbed to the effects of the chloroform, making it effortless to guide her through the ajar bedroom window and into the backseat of his vehicle. He scanned the surroundings to ensure his actions had gone unnoticed before he began his journey back to his laboratory. Thoughts of processing hypotheses churned through his mind as he navigated the road ahead.

Methodically, he laid his latest victim on his operating table and turned on the overhead light. He grabbed a pair of scissors and removed the teenager's clothing. He turned her body over onto her stomach and titled her head to the right. He applied straps to both her arms and legs. He brought over a large stainless steel tray and laid it to the girl's side. Before starting his incision, he turned on some music, Beethoven this time.

After humming a few bars, he injected a high dose of LSD into her arm and then placed smelling salts under her nose. After a few minutes, she began to stir. Frightened and with tears rolling down her cheeks, she tried to free herself from the restraints. The more she struggled, the faster the LSD went through her system.

Dr. Sinclair observed her frantic attempts to scream, but only a strained, guttural sound managed to break free. A fresh expression materialized across her features – precisely what he had anticipated. The manifestation of pure terror. As she writhed face down on the table, he discerned the initial indications of her tingler exerting pressure against the skin veiling her spinal column.

The moment is nearing, Sinclair mused inwardly. With a final arch of her back, her life ebbed away. Swiftly seizing the scalpel, he traced the familiar path down the spinal cord's length. And there it was, frenetically convulsing within the confines of the spleen. Judging its dimensions to be approximately thirteen inches, he carefully excised the spleen, affording him a secure grip on the creature. He deposited it onto the gleaming stainless-steel tray before transferring it to a compact cage, spacious enough for it to traverse and acquaint itself with its unfamiliar surroundings.

With meticulous care, he commenced the task of transcribing his observations into his laboratory journal. Each page bore witness to the groundbreaking revelations, a testament to his dedication. Time slipped through his fingers, and then a realization struck – he needed to inspect Medussa, who had remained unusually subdued. It was then he stumbled upon the shocking truth: she had managed to escape, deftly forcing open the case-hardened steel lid of her enclosure.

CHAPTER

ELEVEN

AFTER REVIEWING THE reports from the graveyard shift on her desk, Sarah rose and indulged in a stretch. Two consecutive nights of restful sleep had been a welcome respite. She filled her cup for the fourth time with coffee and then touched base with Sandy.

"Chief, I've compiled the details you asked for regarding training courses and such. Quite a few caught my interest," Sandy explained, offering a set of printed pages to Sarah. Rather than taking them, Sarah suggested that Sandy initial the specific courses she was interested in. This gesture brought a wide grin to Sandy's face.

Subsequently, she made her way back to her office, the sound of Sandy's voice answering the department's phone trailing behind her. A handful of seconds later, Sandy appeared at the doorway of Sarah's office.

"Chief, Tom Scott from the Raven's Hollow Examiner is on the line for you. Just so you know, he's very handsome in my opinion, but as slippery as an eel if you catch my drift."

"Thank you, Sandy. I'll bear that in mind." Sandy returned to her desk as Sarah readied herself to answer her office phone.

"Chief Morgan speaking. How can I assist you?" she inquired.

"Yes, Chief. My name is Tom Scott, and I'm a reporter with the Raven's Hollow Examiner. I was hoping we could set up a date and time for me to introduce myself and provide you with some insights about our city. Having been born and raised here, I know many of our residents on a first-name basis. Would you be available this afternoon for a meeting?"

While Sarah suspected his underlying intention was to ambush her with questions about the Thompson homicide, she opted to go along with it. "I have some availability at 2 PM today. Does that work for you?"

"Absolutely. I'm looking forward to our meeting then. Thank you, Chief," he replied.

"Chief, this might interest you. The City of Dayton, that's a few miles away, just reported that a young teenage girl has just been reported kidnapped from her bedroom. There's not much here regarding particulars, but I thought you'd want to know," Sandy said as she laid the printout on Sarah's desk.

After quickly scanning the message, Sarah stepped out of her office and headed toward Sandy's desk. "Sandy, do you happen to have the phone number for the Chief of Police in Dayton?"

Within a short period, Sarah found herself on hold after introducing herself to the individual who answered the line at the Dayton Police Department.

"Chief Morgan, a pleasure to meet you, even if it's over the phone. How's everything going in Raven's Hollow?" Chief Jim Osborne inquired once he came on the line.

Sarah responded, "Things are progressing steadily here in Raven's Hollow. I've been getting acquainted with the team and the community." Their conversation flowed naturally, with Chief Osborne sharing some insights about his own experiences as a police chief. After a few minutes, Sarah decided to inquire about a pressing matter.

"I received your broadcast regarding a kidnapping either late last night or early this morning," Sarah began the conversation. "As you're aware, we're currently in the midst of investigating a homicide where a woman was seemingly abducted from her residence, subsequently murdered, and left on Route 81. I was wondering if you could provide some insights about your case. I'm keen on identifying any potential similarities."

"Of course, Chief Morgan," Chief Osborne responded.

"Please, Chief. Call me Sarah."

"Sarah it is. My name is Jim. In our case, the parents of the abducted victim discovered their daughter missing from her bed around 7 in the morning. They immediately searched both the house and the yard, but there was no sign of her. It's crucial to note that she's not the type to run away – this situation is quite out of character for her.

When we arrived at the scene, there was no substantial evidence to be found, except for a distinctive shoe imprint in the soil right outside her bedroom window, which was the apparent point of entry and exit."

Chief Osborne's voice conveyed the weight of the situation. "However, the shoe imprint itself doesn't provide a clear lead. It's an imprint of a size 11 shoe, but there's no discernible tread pattern or unique characteristics. Given that there's no distinct imprint from the shoe, it suggests that it could be either a dress shoe or perhaps the perpetrator used shoe coverings to avoid leaving any telltale marks."

He sighed lightly. "That's about all we have to report at the moment. The circumstances are unsettling similar to your case, and I share your concern regarding these potential connections. If you like, I will forward any progress we make directly to your office."

"Yes, I would Jim. We also found a size 11 shoe imprint outside the bedroom window of our victim. I will put in a request at the forensic lab, if you concur, and see if we have a match."

"That is not a problem. You think we might have a serial on our hands?"

"You never know Jim. I will be in touch."

Sarah's intuition strongly suggested they were dealing with a serial kidnapper, and if the abducted individual from Dayton ended up deceased, it would confirm her suspicions. Yet, a sense of frustration gnawed at her. In all her years as a homicide investigator, it always came down to a single piece of evidence that would lead her in the direction of the suspect. But for now, all she had was a possible similar case in Dayton with two shoe imprints.

Realizing the need for solitude, she resolved to take a few moments to jot down her knowledge and identify the gaps. Hopefully, this introspective exercise would illuminate a path to pursue before more potential victims vanished. Glancing at her watch, she noted that it was nearing 1 pm—a perfect opportunity to grab a burger, fries, and a soda, then retreat to the tranquil park at the heart of the town. As she chewed over her thoughts, the reminder of her 2 pm appointment with Tom Scott surfaced in her mind.

The park was remarkably empty save two children playing on playground equipment at the far end under the watchful eyes of two mothers. Extracting her spiral notebook, she commenced by drawing a vertical line down the center of the page. Under the headings "Thompson" and "Dayton Teenager," Sarah commenced detailing her insights.

Thompson: Aged eighty-two. Widowed. Non-driver. Reclusive, aside from her neighbors. Likely abduction victim, followed by murder. Spleen extracted. Body discarded on highway. Absence of apparent enemies. Probable point of entry: bedroom window. Shoe imprint size: 11.

Dayton Teenager: Nearly eighteen. High school student. No identifiable adversaries. Kidnapped from bedroom during nighttime or early morning hours. Shoe imprint size: 11. Still unlocated.

Sarah reviewed her notes, hoping to glean some revelation. Yet, nothing stood out. Overwhelmed by frustration, she concluded her meal, disposed of her waste in a bin near a water fountain, and retraced her steps to her vehicle.

With her hunger quenched, she walked into her office after grabbing another cup of coffee. Sandy offered a reminder about the impending 2 o'clock appointment with Scott from the Examiner. As the time drew near, Sarah contemplated her approach for the meeting, fully aware of Scott's likely agenda. A lingering thought resurfaced – the mayor's directive to ensure his presence at televised press releases. In the recesses of her mind, she recalled this instruction. Yet, she reasoned that this meeting wasn't a televised event, thus negating the necessity to inform "his honor."

CHAPTER

TWELVE

SARAH HAD HER new office adorned with
official documents, a map of Raven's Hollow, and
a whiteboard covered in case details. Adorning
a different wall hung a proclamation bestowed upon
her by the City of Los Angeles, a testament to her
extensive and distinguished career as a homicide
investigator.

A knock at the door signaled the arrival of Tom
Scott, the curious reporter from the Raven's Hollow
Examiner. With a polite nod, she invited him in,
his presence adding a sense of urgency to the room.
Tom's eyes flickered with a mix of intrigue and
professionalism as he took in his surroundings. Sandy
was right. He was very handsome an in great shape.

"Chief Morgan, I want to thank you for taking the
time out of your schedule to meet with me. I am hoping
on a short interview that I can run in our Sunday
edition where the citizens of Raven's Hollow can read
about the background of their new police chief.

Sarah gestured for him to take a seat, her gaze steady as she leaned forward on her desk. "Mr. Scott," she began, her tone a blend of formality and determination, "That would be a nice piece for your readers and I would be willing to be interviewed, but at least cut to the chase. I know your primary interest is in the Thompson homicide case."

Sarah could sense that she knocked Scott a little off balance. She continued. "You understand I can't divulge much about our investigation since we are in the early stages. What I can tell you is that there are unsettling connections between this recent homicide and some other cases across the county. This investigation goes deeper than what's on the surface."

Tom nodded, his notebook at the ready. "I understand, Chief Morgan. I'm here not only to get a story but to shed light on the truth. If there's anything you can share that might lead us to that truth, it could make a difference."

Sarah studied him for a moment, gauging his sincerity. "Alright, Tom. Let's talk about patterns, secrets, and what's lurking beneath the surface of Raven's Hollow. But remember, off the record for now."

As Sarah and Tom delved into the intricacies of the case, the proclamation on the wall caught his eye. "Impressive," he commented, nodding toward it. "Being recognized by the City of Los Angeles for your work as a decorated homicide investigator – that's quite an achievement, Chief Morgan."

A faint smile played on Sarah's lips as she acknowledged his appreciation. "Thank you, Mr. Scott. It was a chapter of my life I'm proud of." The glint of admiration in Tom's eyes didn't go unnoticed by her. As they exchanged stories and insights, the atmosphere in the room seemed to shift, an unspoken connection forming between them.

As the conversation veered toward a case in Dayton with eerie similarities, Sarah recounted the details she had discovered. Tom leaned forward, genuinely intrigued. "Please, call me Tom. You know," he mused, his voice taking on a more personal tone, "I've been following cases like that, and I've come across at least five others in this county with strikingly similar patterns."

Sarah's interest was piqued. She met his gaze, a silent acknowledgment passing between them. "That's a significant number," she replied, her professional curiosity blending with a growing sense of partnership. "If you have information that could shed light on this investigation, I'd value your input."

Tom's eyes held hers for a lingering moment, his initial flirtatiousness giving way to a more earnest connection. "Chief Morgan, I'd be honored to assist however I can. In fact, there's something else I'd like to propose," he said, a slight hesitation in his voice as he mustered the courage to continue. "Once this conversation concludes, would you consider joining me for a drink? You know, to discuss the case further."

Sarah's heart skipped a beat, a mix of surprise and a warming sense of attraction coursing through her. She considered his offer, her professional façade momentarily melting. "I appreciate your dedication to the truth, Tom," she replied, her tone sincere. "A drink sounds like a good idea. Let's see where this partnership takes us."

"Can I go back on the record, Chief?" Tom's request caught Sarah's attention, and she nodded, curiosity piqued about what new information he was about to unveil. "Sure," she replied, her demeanor poised for whatever curveball he was about to throw.

"What I've gathered from sources across multiple police agencies," Tom began, his tone measured, "is that these victims, including Mrs. Thompson, all had one peculiar commonality: their spleens were surgically removed. And not to mention, they were all mute."

Sarah's practiced composure prevented her surprise from showing, even though this revelation was news to her. She had yet to delve into Mrs. Thompson's mute condition, a detail that had seemingly eluded her. As their conversation continued, a sense of shared purpose and a growing connection between them seemed to permeate the room, bridging the gap between professional collaboration and something more intimate.

"Well, Chief," Tom's voice shifted, a subtle shift in the air suggesting a change in tone, "if you're familiar with the Raven's Hollow hotel downtown, near the bakery, maybe we could meet there at 5. If that suits your schedule."

Sarah's heart fluttered at his proposal, her gaze meeting his with an undeniable spark. She smiled, her professionalism momentarily giving way to a more personal sentiment. "That sounds like a plan, Tom," she responded, the corners of her lips curling upwards. As Tom rose to leave, she couldn't help but notice his parting flirtation with Sandy as he closed the door behind him.

With the weight of the investigation and their burgeoning connection still hanging in the air, Sarah allowed herself a moment of quiet anticipation. The partnership they were forming had the potential to uncover not only the sinister truths hidden within the case but also the deeper emotions that had slowly begun to emerge between them.

CHAPTER

THIRTEEN

FTER TOM SCOTT had left her office, Sarah turned her attention to the file on the Thompson homicide and quickly located Charlotte's phone number. After a few rings, Charlotte picked up the call. "Hello, Charlotte, this is Chief Morgan from the Raven's Hollow Police Department. We spoke yesterday with Officer Stansberry. I have a follow-up question I'd like to ask you, if you're available."

"Oh, hello Chief Morgan. Yes, I remember you and the charming officer who was with you," Charlotte replied warmly. "How can I assist you?"

Sarah cleared her throat, preparing to ask the crucial question. "Charlotte, I wanted to inquire whether Mrs. Thompson was a deaf mute?"

Charlotte's response initially felt like a weight dropping in Sarah's chest. "No," she said, shattering the possibility of a potential lead. "One minute Chief, I need to help my husband. I will be right back." After a few seconds she did return. "No, she could hear perfectly well but she had been mute since birth."

Shortly after, Sarah initiated calls to the police chiefs and sheriffs of the neighboring jurisdictions. In a synchronized chorus, each confirmed the unsettling trend: a series of open cases involving identified and unidentified bodies, all being discarded as trash, all mute, and all having their spleens removed. A disconcerting commonality was emerging. Astonishingly, this crucial detail had slipped through the cracks of prior investigations.

With a sense of urgency, Sarah's interactions with the various law enforcement agencies unveiled a shared vow to rectify their oversights. Each promised swift cooperation, pledging to transmit their findings to her without delay.

"Sandy," Sarah's voice echoed through the office intercom, "Could you spare a moment?"

"Certainly, Chief. What can I assist you with?" came Sandy's prompt response. Stepping into Sarah's office, she awaited instructions.

Providing Sandy with a comprehensive update, Sarah detailed the troubling revelation that had come to light. The victims' shared affliction of muteness was now the linchpin of their investigation. As baffling as it was, this recurring trait seemed to hold a crucial significance—though the purpose remained enigmatic.

With the pieces of this macabre puzzle slowly assembling, Chief Sarah Morgan and her team were determined to uncover the insidious motivations lurking behind the abductions. The chilling realization that mute victims stood as the common thread only intensified their pursuit of the truth, as they delved deeper into the darkness that gripped Raven's Hollow.

"As these reports begin to arrive, I'd like you to thoroughly review each one, keeping an eye out for any additional shared characteristics beyond their muteness. Look into whether they attended the same church, school, or clubs—anything that might link them. I understand you already have your front office responsibilities, so if delving into this requires extra time, don't hesitate to put in overtime."

"You once mentioned that someday you wanted to become a police officer. Well, here's your opportunity to step into that role, detective," Sarah quipped with a wink, strolling back toward her office.

Dr. Sinclair's cell phone vibrated insistently on his lab table, signaling the arrival of a new text message. The words on the screen posed a question: "Why did you choose to abduct such a young woman?" His initial impulse was to ignore it, dismissing any audacity to question his groundbreaking pursuits. Yet, the persistent inquiry managed to provoke a response from him.

Defiance mingled with a begrudging curiosity as he eventually typed out a reply: "Our aim is to determine the precise threshold at which a tingler can induce fatal terror in a subject. The specimen I extracted from her exhibits remarkable growth—thanks to my proprietary growth hormone, it's already increased by an inch." A sense of satisfaction accompanied his decision to send the message.

The seconds stretched out as Dr. Sinclair awaited a response. A subsequent text message illuminated the screen: "Your discovery is indeed remarkable but be wary. The authorities are in a frenzy over the missing teenagers. I trust you've erased any trace of your involvement, and mine." Sinclair briefly pondered whether to bring up the escape of Medusa, yet he ultimately concluded that the creature had likely sought refuge within a storm drain and met its death.

Annette was nestled close to her husband, her body pressed tightly against his. The creature on the screen possessed the uncanny ability to blend seamlessly with the jungle's fauna. Some scenes of the movie were so gripping that she found herself burying her head into her husband's chest for refuge. Unbeknownst to her, Medussa was stealthily crawling down the aisle, drawn directly toward her exposed leg that extended into its path.

Much like the menacing creature in the Predator film, which stood poised on a fallen log in its pursuit of Schwarzenegger's hidden character, Annette once more sought refuge by burying her head in Dennis's chest. In eerie synchrony, just as the tension escalated on screen, Medusa's grip fastened around Annette's leg, constricting with a suffocating force. Annette's shrill screams echoed, intertwining with the chorus of terrified voices in the audience, mirroring the unfolding scene before them.

The collective cacophony of screams reverberated through the theater, casting an immediate impact on Medusa. The creature's size visibly diminished, halving itself in response to the wave of screams unleashed by the audience. Relinquishing its hold on Annette's leg, Medusa hastily retreated along the path it had initially entered, vanishing into the shadows.

Sarah reached the hotel for her scheduled meeting with Tom Scott. She managed to squeeze in a quick visit to her B&B to apply a touch of perfume and freshen up. She also took a moment to inform the manager of her impending departure the following day for her new residence. She felt nervous since she realized this was the first 'date' since the loss of her husband and daughter.

The police department's shrink collaborated with Sarah over the course of several months after the tragedy that claimed her family. Eventually, the therapist advised Sarah to find a way to bring closure to that painful chapter of her life, a task that Sarah found exceptionally challenging.

Upon entering the bar, Tom caught her attention from a corner booth, and greeted her with a wave. Making her way toward him, Sarah noticed he retained the same attire as earlier in her office, projecting a gentlemanly demeanor.

After settling into her seat, Tom signaled for the server's attention. The young hostess approached with a friendly smile. "Hello there, what can I get for you?" she inquired.

"I'll have a Vodka martini on the rocks," Sarah replied. The hostess turned her attention to Tom, who ordered a second Vodka Collins.

"So, Sarah, how did the rest of your day unfold?" Tom inquired.

"Thanks to your insights, we managed to explore some new avenues," Sarah responded. She appreciated the opportunity to expand on the progress they had made earlier.

"Oh, really. Could you elaborate?" Tom inquired further.

Initially, Sarah hesitated before responding. "Tom, as a police officer, you understand the constraints around discussing ongoing investigations. However, your observation about the victims being mute and having their spleens removed aligns with our own homicide case. Additionally, I've verified that similar cases exist in other jurisdictions beyond our county."

She continued, her tone cautionary, "But before you rush to disseminate the possibility of a serial killer to the citizens of Raven's Hollow and the neighboring areas, I need to issue a warning. If you ever compromise my trust, you'll lose the privilege of interviewing me again. Let me emphasize that the mayor's priority, as soon as he heard about our homicide, was to insist on his presence during any television interviews.

"Now, considering I don't spot any television cameras here in the bar, I'm inclined to believe I'm not infringing on his mandate," she quipped with a smile, savoring a sip of her martini while awaiting his response.

In response, Tom playfully uttered a single word, "Ouch," his eyes locked onto Sarah's as he raised his drink to his lips. He then met her gaze with a sincere expression, continuing, "Sarah, let me assure you, I'd never jeopardize our professional relationship. This city might be small, but my commitment to being an effective reporter for the Examiner is paramount. And yes, I sense there might be a connection between us, though I want to clarify it's not a come-on. I'm sure Sandy warned you to keep an eye out for me."

"Why on earth would Sandy mention something like that?" Sarah retorted, her response betraying a hint of reluctance to acknowledge that she was indeed privy to such advice.

"Sandy and I had a brief relationship, around two or three years ago. She had aspirations of traveling before fully committing to her studies. Back then, my career at the Examiner was just gaining momentum, and I couldn't exactly drop everything to jet off to Rome or Paris. That's when we started growing apart. Despite that, we've remained good friends. But all of that is in the past now," Tom explained.

"And what about you? I'm guessing you've been married before. If you're comfortable sharing, what happened?" Tom inquired respectfully. Sarah finished her drink and motioned to the hostess for a refill.

"I began to share my life story back at the station. During my time with the LAPD, I was involved in the pursuit of a serial killer. My pursuit grew too relentless, and in retaliation, he targeted my family – my husband and our four-year-old daughter. One late night when I returned home from work, I discovered them on the floor of our living room," she recounted, her voice faltering as the weight of her words threatened to overwhelm her. She took a moment, steadying herself with a sip from her drink, her emotions held back behind a mask of composure.

Tom leaned back in his chair, his eyes locked onto Sarah's with a mixture of understanding and empathy. He tore off a piece of the warm bread twist and dipped it into the fragrant olive oil, buying himself a moment to gather his thoughts.

"You're talking about justice that goes beyond the law," he finally said, his voice quiet but firm. "It's about something deeper, something that doesn't always fit within the confines of a courtroom."

Sarah nodded, appreciating Tom's grasp of her unspoken words. "Exactly. Sometimes the system fails, and we're left with a need for closure that's impossible to achieve through official channels."

Their conversation was laden with unspoken emotions, the weight of shared experiences hanging in the air. As they continued to dip bread into the oil, a sense of camaraderie began to develop between them, a connection forged through their shared determination to uncover the truth.

"Sarah," Tom said after a pause, "I can't promise you swift justice for your past, but I can promise you this: I'll do everything in my power to shine a light on the darkness that's lurking in our town. Those who believe they're beyond the reach of justice need to be reminded that their actions have consequences."

CHAPTER

FOURTEEN

AS THE LATE afternoon gradually transitioned into evening, Tom managed to persuade Sarah to let him treat her to dinner at the hotel's restaurant. It was a chance to allow the effects of their drinks to wear off while also relishing each other's company.

They settled into a cozy corner of the restaurant, the soft glow of ambient lighting casting a warm atmosphere. The clinking of cutlery and distant murmurs of other diners created a comforting backdrop.

"I must admit, Sarah," Tom began, unfolding his napkin with a playful glint in his eyes, "you have a way of taking charge, even when circumstances are far from ordinary."

Sarah chuckled softly, her eyes meeting his with a mix of amusement and appreciation. "It's a skill I've honed over time. Sometimes, in a world that's constantly shifting, taking charge is the only way to navigate through the chaos."

Tom nodded, their easy rapport creating a sense of camaraderie that felt almost effortless. He scanned the menu briefly before setting it aside. "Speaking of chaos, it seems our town has its own share of mysteries."

Sarah's expression grew serious as she leaned in slightly, a glint of determination in her eyes. "Indeed. And I'm not one to back down from a challenge, especially when it comes to uncovering the truth."

Their conversation flowed seamlessly as they discussed their town, its history, and the deep-seated secrets that seemed to permeate every corner. Sarah used the opportunity to turn the intimate dinner atmosphere back towards work.

Their words intertwined effortlessly as they explored the intricacies of their town, delving into its history and the hidden enigmas that seemed to lurk around every corner. Amid the shared laughter and anecdotes, Sarah saw a chance to gracefully steer the conversation back to matters at hand.

As a lull settled over their delightful exchange, Sarah's gaze met Tom's, her expression thoughtful yet curious. "Tom," she began, her tone casual yet purposeful, "you mentioned earlier that you're a native of Raven' Hollow. Could you shed some light on this intriguing 'Fearmonger' legend that I've caught glimpses of?"

Tom's eyes flickered with recognition, a mixture of curiosity and caution dancing within them. It was as if the very mention of the myth held a certain weight, a significance that couldn't be ignored. He took a sip of his wine, his expression turning contemplative.

"The 'Fearmonger,' Sarah," Tom started, his voice steady, "is a tale that's been woven into the fabric of this town for generations. It's said to be a specter, an entity that feeds on fear itself. Whispers in the shadows suggest that it preys on those who are burdened by guilt, haunting their minds until their fear consumes them."

Sarah's interest was piqued, her curiosity mingling with a hint of skepticism. "A supernatural legend? That's quite the story to have persisted over the years."

Tom nodded, his gaze fixed on some distant memory. "Indeed. Some dismiss it as nothing more than a campfire tale, while others claim to have felt its presence in the dead of night."

Sarah's fingers idly traced the rim of her wineglass, her thoughts churning. "And do you believe in this 'Fearmonger,' Tom? Is it a manifestation of genuine fear or just a reflection of the darkness that can take root in people's minds?"

Tom's smile was rueful as he met Sarah's gaze once again. "Sarah, in a town like Raven's Hollow, where secrets seem to be buried as deeply as the roots of our oldest trees, anything is possible. Whether the 'Fearmonger' is real or not, its legend reflects the very real fears that can grip a person's heart."

Their conversation had shifted from light-hearted camaraderie to a more introspective exploration of the human psyche. As the evening continued to unfold, Sarah couldn't help but wonder if the 'Fearmonger' might hold a key to the mysteries that had begun to unravel around them.

Tom discreetly retrieved an article from his pocket, his thumb grazing its edges. Originally intending to share it with Sarah on a more opportune occasion, he realized that the current atmosphere was conducive to their ongoing discussion. As the thread of their dinner conversation wove back to work-related matters, he recognized it was the right moment to reveal this particular piece of information.

"Sarah," he began, a tone of cautious anticipation in his voice, "there's something I've been meaning to show you. It's related to the topic at hand." Sarah's curiosity was immediately piqued. She regarded Tom with a mixture of intrigue and openness, ready to absorb whatever he was about to present.

"Has anyone on your team mentioned the events that supposedly transpired here in 1959?" Tom asked, his eyes locking onto Sarah's, gauging her reaction.

"No," Sarah replied. That was before they were born, so if they knew anything if had to be passed down to them."

As Sarah leaned forward, her eyes fixed on the article Tom had retrieved, a hushed anticipation settled between them. He unfolded the aged paper, the yellowed edges revealing its history. In faded black print, the headline told a story that had lingered in the shadows of Raven' Hollow's past.

"On August 3, 1959," Tom began, his voice carrying a touch of gravity, "an incident occurred that left its mark on the town's history." He cleared his throat and continued, "A young woman and her friend attended a silent movie screening at the historic theater, the Avalon, downtown. As she became engrossed in the film, something extraordinary happened."

Sarah's attention sharpened as she listened intently, her mind conjuring images of a bygone era and the eerie allure of silent cinema.

"According to the article," Tom recounted, "the woman claimed that during the movie, she felt a peculiar sensation on her leg. She described it as a giant insect, crawling up her leg with a grip so tight that her leg began to numb from lack of blood circulation."

As Tom's words wove the tale, Sarah's expression shifted from curiosity to a mixture of fascination and intrigue. The setting, the ambiance of the old theater, and the bizarre incident combined to create an atmosphere of surreal mystery.

"With a jolt of fear, she screamed as loudly as she could," Tom continued, his voice echoing the shock of that long-ago night, "and in response, the creature— whatever it was—released her leg and scuttled away."

The weight of the story hung in the air as Tom lowered the article, allowing the words to linger between them. Sarah's thoughts raced, attempting to grasp the significance of this peculiar event and its potential relevance to their current investigation.

After a moment of quiet contemplation, Sarah broke the silence. "Tom, did anyone follow up on this woman's story? Did the police investigate further?"

Tom's expression turned somber, his gaze distant. "No. The police arrived at the scene, but by that point, no trace of the insect or whatever it was could be found. As time passed, the incident became more of a local legend, something that people would tell with a mix of amusement and skepticism. Who knows. Maybe that is where the whole 'Fearmonger' legend came from."

Sarah's brow furrowed, a blend of curiosity and determination creasing her features. "If this woman's account holds any truth, it could potentially tie into the events unfolding now. I can't help but wonder if she's still alive, living here in the city."

Tom nodded in agreement, his eyes reflecting a shared sense of urgency. "I can make it a priority to check first thing tomorrow morning. I'll gather whatever information I can find and bring it to the station. Additionally, I'll delve into our microfilm archives, see if there are any other stories that might shed light on this."

Their conversation had ventured deep into the realm of historical intrigue, a search for connections that spanned decades. As the evening waned and the restaurant's ambiance enveloped them, Sarah and Tom were united by a shared mission—to unravel the past in order to illuminate the present and safeguard the future.

As dessert arrived, Sarah found herself grateful for this unexpected companionship. The evening had turned out to be much more than a way to sober up—it had become a moment of respite, a brief escape from the weight of their responsibilities.

Tom's eyes met Sarah's, his smile warm and genuine. He reached across the table and held one of Sarah's hands. In return, she caressed his hand. "Sarah, I'm glad we had this chance to share a meal and our thoughts. I hope, in some small way, it's brought you a sense of camaraderie."

Sarah raised her glass of water in a quiet toast. "To camaraderie, Tom. In a world that often feels fragmented, it's a precious gift."

CHAPTER

FIFTEEN

D ESPITE THE HOURS that had passed, Sarah's energy remained unwavering as she returned to the cozy B&B. With swift efficiency, she loaded her car with the essentials for her impending move, leaving out only what she needed for the next day—her chosen attire and toiletries. She had a plan in mind—to pay a visit to her new home and meet with the sellers. The goal: to obtain her keys and initiate the process of making the house her own.

Another night of restlessness awaited Sarah, yet this time her usual nightmares were notably absent. The Valium, as recommended by Chelsea, seemed to be delivering its intended effect. However, despite the absence of haunting dreams, her mind refused to quiet. It raced through a spectrum of thoughts, spanning from the impending move scheduled for the next day to the enigmatic 'Fearmonger' legend, and even the harrowing encounter with the colossal insect at the town's historic theater back in 1959.

A multitude of unanswered questions loomed before her, a seemingly overwhelming puzzle to piece together. The weight of these uncertainties felt almost insurmountable for a single individual to tackle. As she contemplated the complexities of the situation, a glimmer of hope emerged. Sarah found herself hoping that Tom's expressed commitment to utilizing his resources wasn't merely a passing sentiment. Only time would reveal the sincerity of his intentions, and she was prepared to gauge that in due course.

Having her car meticulously packed, Sarah settled her final bill and expressed her gratitude to the proprietors of the B&B. With her departure imminent, she set out to rendezvous with the sellers at her eagerly awaited new home. The scene that greeted her was a pleasant surprise—an amiable reception awaited her, complete with open arms and a homemade "Welcome Home" cake. This thoughtful gesture, unlike something store-bought, caught her off guard. As they exchanged pleasantries, keys were handed over, solidifying her entrance into this new chapter of her life.

Swiftly depositing her belongings in the front room, Sarah's mind buzzed with anticipation for the process of unpacking that lay ahead. Yet, there was a more immediate delight to share. She seized the "Welcome Home" cake, a symbol of the warm welcome she had received, and headed to the police department. In her heart, she hoped to find Sandy preparing a pot of coffee, a comforting undercurrent in the hustle and bustle of the day.

Entering the station's lobby, Sarah was greeted by a pleasantly unexpected sight—Sandy, with a warm smile, indicated Tom's presence. He was engrossed in his cell phone until her arrival prompted him to stow it in his jacket pocket, his expression transforming into a broad grin of welcome.

Teasingly, Tom quipped, "You know, you really didn't need to go through the trouble of baking a cake just for me." Sandy's reaction was an eye roll, an amused yet familiar response.

With a playful glint in her eye, Sarah extended an invitation, her voice carrying a note of camaraderie, "If coffee and cake sound appealing, follow me." Leading the way, she guided both Tom and Sandy to the breakroom, where a blend of lighthearted conversation and shared moments awaited.

After assembling paper plates, forks, and a serving knife, Sarah deftly cut portions of cake for everyone present. With the desserts prepared, she extended an invitation to Tom, suggesting they continue their conversation in her office. He excused himself briefly, remembering his forgotten briefcase in the lobby.

Upon his return, he set down his cake slice and coffee cup on Sarah's desk before pulling out a laptop from his briefcase. Drawing his chair closer to her desk, he leaned forward, his expression taking on a seriousness that captured her attention.

"Since our dinner last night, I've been delving into some research," Tom began, his tone measured yet resolute. "And I've stumbled upon something that might hold significance for our investigation."

Intrigued, Sarah leaned in, her curiosity kindled. "Please, go on."

The laptop's screen illuminated with a series of news articles, each headline telling a story of its own. Tom's voice held a note of gravity as he explained, "Five disturbingly similar murders have occurred in the surrounding counties over the past year. In each case, the victims were kidnapped, and their spleens were surgically removed."

Sarah's eyes widened as she absorbed the chilling information before her. "And these victims, they were all mute?"

Tom nodded, his expression mirroring the weight of the revelation. "Yes, Chief. Each one seemed to have been silenced before their deaths, as if there's a deliberate effort to suppress their voices."

As the pieces of this unsettling puzzle began to connect, Sarah's mind worked furiously to grasp the implications. "There's a pattern here, Tom. But why mute victims? What could possibly link these cases?"

Leaning back in his chair, Tom considered her questions thoughtfully. "I don't have all the answers yet. But I'm determined to uncover the truth. There's a dark undercurrent at play, and I believe it's connected to more than just the surface."

His resolve evident, Tom continued with a new layer of information. "Digging further, I went back to August 1959, and I found a few articles related to the incident at the Avalon—the insect attack you mentioned. While many of the articles dismissed it as sensationalism or far-fetched claims like creatures from outer space, I managed to find one consistent detail. The name of the alleged victim was Dorothy Cummings."

"Is she still with us?" Sarah inquired, her curiosity tinged with a sense of urgency.

Tom's smile held a touch of anticipation, as though he had foreseen her question. "Indeed, she's in her nineties now, residing at Meadow Brook Rest Home on the south side of the city. I assume you're considering paying her a visit?"

Sarah's lips curved into a smile, appreciating Tom's ability to anticipate her thoughts. "Great minds do think alike. But before you go anywhere, let's finish our cake and coffee."

The air held a sense of purpose, as they shared not only information but also a mutual determination to seek answers. In the quiet of Sarah's office, a turning point had been reached—one that might shed light on both the history and the present challenges they faced.

CHAPTER

SIXTEEN

S ARAH COULDN'T HELP but feel a sense
of awe as she took in the car that Tom drove.
Though pre-owned, the sight of a three-year-old
Ferrari was quite the spectacle. Amusement danced in
her eyes as she turned to him, a playful remark on her
lips as they set off for the rest home.

"Must be some impressive perks in the world of
news reporting to afford a car like that," she quipped,
a smile playing on her face.

"After my parents passed away, and with no
siblings, their house and savings turned into quite an
inheritance," Tom explained, a mix of nostalgia and
practicality in his tone. "I already had a place to call
home, so a significant portion went into savings and
investments. And, well, the rest went towards a bit of
indulgence for myself. Though I must admit, driving
this car on long trips can be quite impractical. But
moments like today, cruising through the countryside
with a captivating woman by my side—well, it feels
like living the dream."

A smile tugged at Sarah's lips as she absorbed his candid explanation. "You certainly have a way with words, don't you?" she quipped, her eyes sparkling with amusement.

Meadow Brook Senior Residence embodied the quintessential image of an elderly care facility. A carefully constructed stream, complete with a gentle waterfall, originated at one end of the entrance and meandered gracefully around its perimeter. Immaculately maintained lawns played host to landscaping that harmoniously enhanced the charm of the one-story, soft yellow façade.

"Hello, I'm Chief Sarah Morgan representing the Raven's Hollow Police Department. While we don't have a scheduled appointment, if it's possible, we would appreciate the opportunity to see Dorothy Cummings."

After a swift appraisal of the two visitors, the receptionist, displaying a rather distant demeanor, tapped a few keys on her computer. "Dorothy currently occupies room 207. She's scheduled for physical therapy at 10 am, followed by lunch. You'll have approximately an hour to visit. Take the left corridor, and upon reaching the first junction, make a right turn. The room number is positioned beside the entrance."

As they walked down the hallway, Sarah reminded Tom that technically this was part of a homicide investigation and anything they learned from Ms.

Cummings, needed to be cleared by Sarah before it could be published. Tom understood.

The open door led them into the room, where two women lay in their beds. Sarah and Tom faced a challenge, not being familiar with what Dorothy looked like in 1959, let alone in the present day.

"Who are you looking for?" the woman closest to the door inquired, her voice resonating loudly enough to rouse the other woman from her slumber.

"Hello," Sarah greeted. "We're here to see Dorothy Cummings."

A faint voice responded, "I'm Dorothy. How can I help you?"

Sarah and Tom approached Dorothy's bedside. With only a single chair available, Tom gestured for Sarah to occupy it. Sarah presented her badge to Cummings, saying, "Dorothy, my name is Sarah Morgan, and I've taken on the role of Police Chief for Raven's Hollow."

Cummings reached for her nightstand, donned a pair of glasses, and examined Sarah's badge. "I used to live in Raven's Hollow," she reflected, her gaze drifting towards the adjacent window. "My husband, may he rest in peace, spent many years there."

Her thoughts wandered as she fixated on the distant view beyond the window. "Dorothy, would it be acceptable if I referred to you as Dorothy?" Sarah inquired.

"Why not? That's her damn name, isn't it?," a voice chimed in from the neighboring bed.

Recognizing the need to engage the other woman, Tom subtly indicated his intention, effectively diverting her attention.

"Well, well, aren't you a handsome devil?" Sarah overheard the woman comment as Tom approached her bedside. Shifting her focus back to Dorothy, Sarah continued, "Dorothy, do you remember the incident at the old movie theater called the Avalon?"

"Avalon? I used to go there for silent movies. It's where Fred and I had our first date. He was quite the scoundrel, always trying to get a little too close," Dorothy shared, her eyes welling with memories that led her to avert her gaze toward the window.

"You know," she resumed, returning to the present moment, "I was attacked there by this massive creature. It tried to rip my leg off."

"That's what I want to talk to you about. What do you recall about the creature? What did it look like? What happened since there are not a lot of reports in the newspapers from back then?"

"What time is it? You know lunch is scheduled for 11 am. Today, they're serving grilled cheese sandwiches and tomato soup. Or was that what I had yesterday?" She paused, her recollections muddled. "There was this enormous worm-like thing with claws and a gaping mouth that climbed up my leg. I was certain it couldn't be Fred because he was on the other side."

A frown etched across her face as she strained to retrieve the memory in detail. "The whole audience was in stitches at the movie. I can't quite recall its title, but it was a real gem. I laughed, Fred laughed. That's when he attempted to slide his hand towards my breast, that old goat. But then, I felt these small hands on the outer side of my left leg. Many legs, in fact.

The room had just enough light for me to discern the creature's outline. It gazed up at me and with its pincers—yes, that's right, it had pincers instead of a mouth—it latched onto my leg. Oh, the pain was so great. I tried to shove it away but its gripe got tighter and tighter. Finally. I screamed as loud as I could and it just fell off. I almost climbed into Fred's lap I was so frightened. He asked me what was wrong. I tried to tell him, but I kept screaming. Everyone else in the theater was laughing at the movie." Again, Dorothy drifted off.

"Dorothy, on that night, did you or Fred contact the police?"

"Police? Aren't you the police?" she responded, her confusion evident.

"Yes, I'm the Chief of Police now, but I'm asking if you or Fred called the police when the worm or creature attacked you?"

"I believe we did," she pondered. "He was a kind police officer. There weren't many policewomen back then. He jotted down what I explained had happened. By that time the movie ended, and everyone was leaving except for Fred and me. I remember he scanned the entire aisle, but he didn't find anything.

Initially, Fred thought it might have been some failed movie prank until he and the officer saw the marks on my leg."

"How would you estimate the length of the creature on your leg?"

"Length?" Dorothy questioned.

"Yes, Dorothy. What length are we talking about? Six inches? A foot?"

Dorothy shut her eyes momentarily, causing Sarah to fear she had lost her attention. Then, Dorothy's eyes opened again. "It was at least a foot, perhaps even two feet. It was the most frightening thing I've ever laid eyes on."

Sarah thanked Dorothy for her time. Tom began to leave the bed side of the other elderly woman. "Hey, sonny. If you comeback tonight, I will leave the door open."

CHAPTER

SEVENTEEN

W ELL, IT LOOKS like you have a hot date all lined up for tonight," a joking Sarah said as they made their way back to Tom's Ferrari.

"What can I say? When you got it, you got it?" he replied earning a smack on his shoulder from Sarah.

So, any revelations from Dorothy?" Tom inquired, his car roaring to life as he exited the parking lot.

"Interestingly enough, both yes and no. In the midst of her memory lapses, she managed to share a truly odd and bizarre account of that night at the movie theater," Sarah recounted, relaying the narrative she had received from Dorothy. Captivated, Tom refrained from interrupting, wholly engrossed in the unfolding tale.

With the story concluded, Sarah posed the question, "So, what's your take on this?"

Tom responded, "Sounds like yet another chapter in the 'Fearmonger' saga."

Once again, Sarah playfully thumped Tom's right shoulder. "Get serious. Even if we consider Dorothy's dementia, her recollection of the events held a remarkable clarity. Something genuinely happened to her that night. Although wrapping my head around the idea of this colossal worm-like entity is an entirely different challenge."

Tom pulled up to Sarah's office, bringing the car to a halt. Sarah assured him that he needn't bother opening her car door as she was aware he had to head to the Examiner. Before parting, she extended an invitation for him to join her at her new house for dinner – a casual affair, featuring pizza and a six-pack of beer, while helping her unpack some of her stuff. The simplicity of the plan appealed to Tom, who welcomed the invitation with enthusiasm, responding that he'd be there with bells on.

The moment Sarah stepped into the lobby, an unspoken tension settled over the atmosphere like a heavy shroud. She could practically feel it in the air, a palpable unease that seemed to emanate from every corner. Following Sandy's gaze, her eyes locked onto Mayor Wadsworth, standing by the window, his stern expression fixed on Tom's red Ferrari as it pulled away. In that charged moment, it was as if the room held its breath, the scene setting the stage for an impending showdown between Sarah and the mayor, the undercurrent of conflict simmering just beneath the surface.

The mayor entered Sarah's office, his presence adding a weight to the room that was impossible to ignore. Without skipping a beat, he delved into the heart of the matter. "Sarah," he began, his tone measured but with a hint of sternness, "I couldn't help but notice your apparent closeness with a certain member of the media. You do realize, I assume, that any interactions between the press and our department that are to be televised require my presence?"

Sarah met his gaze head-on, her professionalism unwavering. "Mayor Wadsworth, I'm well aware of the protocol," she responded evenly. "However, the recent developments in the Thompson homicide case have taken us down unexpected paths. The involvement of the reporter is not part of a televised interview; rather, it's a strategic move related to the investigation itself."

The mayor's brows furrowed, skepticism apparent in his expression. "Bringing a reporter into an ongoing investigation, Sarah? That's a bold step. Care to explain?"

Sarah leaned forward, her confidence apparent as she maintained eye contact. "Tom Scott, the reporter in question, has become an invaluable source of information. His insights have shed light on angles we hadn't considered. In fact, I believe his input might be the breakthrough we've been searching for. This is about pursuing justice, Mayor, and I'm willing to explore unconventional avenues to achieve that."

The mayor's concern deepened, his grip on the situation tightening. "I understand your dedication to this case, but we must also consider the bigger picture," he cautioned. "If any of this sensitive information were to leak, it could spell disaster for the Dreamscape development. We're on the cusp of something transformative for our town, and any negative publicity could set us back."

Sarah leaned back, her resolve unwavering. "Mayor, I assure you that I'm well aware of the stakes. I've carefully calculated the risks versus the potential rewards. Our priority is justice, yes, but I also understand the significance of Dreamscape for Raven's Hollow. Rest assured, I'm treading cautiously while utilizing every resource available to crack this case wide open."

The tension in the room seemed to swell, each word exchanged carrying the weight of their differing perspectives. As they locked eyes, it became evident that this conversation was only the beginning of a complex negotiation between Sarah's pursuit of justice and the mayor's concerns for the town's future.

"Would you like an update on the progress of the Thompson case?" Sarah inquired.

"Of course," Wadsworth answered.

"The investigation into her homicide has revealed a disturbing pattern," Sarah replied, her tone measured yet revealing the gravity of the situation. The mayor's composure wavered, his astonishment palpable. "Her homicide is just one of many by presumably the same suspect.

"My God. This situation keeps taking unexpected turns. Are you suggesting that Raven's Hollow has a serial killer on the loose?" He reached for his handkerchief, hastily wiping away sweat from his forehead and under his nose.

"Not at the moment. Our focus is primarily on the Thompson case. However, it's worth noting that neighboring jurisdictions are dealing with a minimum of five cases that share a similar modus operandi," Sarah explained.

"So, if the city council raises questions, we can confidently state that we're not facing a serial killer situation within Raven's Hollow. And, if need be, we could suggest that the suspect's activities seem more centered in other cities?" the mayor proposed.

Sarah allowed a moment of silence to linger, letting his words hang in the air. Sensing his unease in grappling with the potential reality of a serial killer operating within his jurisdiction, she chose to transition to a different topic, steering the conversation away from its unsettling path.

"Mayor, you're undoubtedly aware that a homicide investigation demands an extensive amount of dedicated effort and puts a significant strain on our available manpower," Sarah addressed him, pausing briefly. She chose her words carefully, intending to corner him strategically. "With your consent, I'm considering the option of presenting this matter before the city council. It would involve requesting an increase in our overtime allowance and potentially expanding our officer count.

This situation presents an opportunity for us to make a compelling case. In the event the council proves unyielding, we could subtly hint at the potential gravity of our circumstances – the looming specter of a serial killer within our grasp. It might be worth noting how the citizens of Raven's Hollow would react upon learning that the city council had denied the request of both the mayor and the new Chief of Police."

Her words hung in the air, each sentence a carefully laid piece of her argument. She allowed the weight of her proposal to settle before continuing the discussion, her intent clear: to gain the resources necessary for the investigation while also leveraging the potential fear of a serial killer to her advantage.

Sarah's proposal hung in the air, the room enveloped in a brief silence as the mayor processed her words. His expression seemed thoughtful, contemplative, as he weighed the implications of her strategy. Then, a spark of inspiration ignited within him, and he sat up a little straighter.

"You know, Chief Morgan," he began, his tone carrying a newfound determination, "you've hit upon something truly ingenious. You should consider politics when you decide to retire. The city council does need to be aware of the demands and challenges our police force faces, especially during a critical investigation. It's time they truly grasp the commitment our officers put into ensuring Raven's Hollow remains safe."

Sarah knew that was all bullshit, that the mayor was processing a way to make this a win-win proposition. He leaned forward, his eyes meeting hers, a spark of conviction in his gaze. "I think I'll take it upon myself to personally notify the city council about the situation. You have my full support, and we will work together to ensure our department receives the resources it needs."

The mayor's demeanor exuded a sense of ownership over the idea, as if he had seamlessly taken it to heart and made it his own. "Chief Morgan, proceed with your plan," he declared with a newfound sense of resolve. "If the need arises, I'll be there to back you up every step of the way."

Sarah couldn't help but be impressed by the mayor's swift transformation. She recognized his ability to turn a suggestion into his own initiative, and the realization that they were on the same page brought a sense of satisfaction. With the mayor's endorsement firmly in place, she knew that her pursuit of justice, coupled with the resources required, was now significantly more attainable.

Without saying goodbye, the mayor left the office like a man on a mission. Sandy entered her office. "How did that go if you don't mind me asking?"

"Do you want to be a police officer for the City of Raven's Hollow?"

CHAPTER

EIGHTEEN

S ITUATED ON MAIN Street, the Avalon
Theater bore historical significance. Under
the stewardship of Oliver Higgins and his wife
Martha for an extended period, the theater had
been a haven for cinematic treasures of the Silent
Era. Its screens had illuminated the iconic personas
of Charlie Chaplin, Douglass Fairbanks, Mary
Pickford, alongside the illustrious Greta Garbo and
Lon Chaney.

Following the passing of the Higgins', the theater
lay dormant for years, neglected by the absence of
a rightful heir. Eventually, recognizing its historical
value, the city of Raven's Hollow stepped in,
designating it as a historic landmark. The theater
transitioned into municipal ownership, with city
employees at the helm. They collaborated with junior
college drama students, providing them a platform
for nightly screenings – albeit now featuring more
contemporary films.

Annette Hartman and her husband, Dennis, arrived at the theater early since they wanted to buy a large popcorn with extra butter as well as an extra-large diet Coke which they would share. As Annette and Dennis stood patiently in line for their tickets, they remained oblivious to a glistening trail winding its way around the theater's side and down an alley, leading toward the fire exit.

They easily found their favorite seats near the aisle so Annette could stretch out her left leg after having another knee surgery.

Tonight's showing was an Arnold Swartsnegger's film of 1987, Predator. In it, Arnold, a soldier of fortune, is hired by the U.S. government to secretly rescue a group of politicians trapped in Guatemala. But when he and his team, which included a weapons expert and a CIA agent, land in Central America, something is gravely wrong. After finding a string of dead bodies, the crew discovers they are being hunted by a brutal creature with superhuman strength and the ability to camouflage itself in the flora of the jungle.

Tom arrived in casual attire, ready to assist Sarah with unpacking some of her belongings. Their first order of business was to indulge in the recently delivered pizza while sharing a cold drink. Amidst light conversation, Sarah transitioned to more pressing matters, revealing that neighboring jurisdictions had started sending over their homicide and missing person reports.

As they delved into the details, Sandy's investigation mirrored what Tom and Sarah had already uncovered. The victims shared the same disturbing patterns: abductions, removal of spleens, and haphazard disposals. However, despite her diligent efforts, Sandy had yet to unearth any significant connections. There were no discernible links in terms of churches, clubs, or hobbies. The disheartening reality was that her meticulous search seemed to be yielding no fruitful insights.

With most of the pizza now consumed, Tom and Sarah shifted their focus to the task at hand. Sarah would hand Tom an article, detailing where it should be placed, as they worked to organize her belongings. Amidst the lively banter, jokes, and playful exchanges, Sarah began to feel a sense of contentment, the feeling of being truly at home now settling within her.

As Sarah finished her last beer, a subtle buzz coursed through her, the culmination of a demanding day at work followed by the arduous process of unpacking. Even as fleeting thoughts of intimacy with Tom crossed her mind amidst the scattered boxes and discarded wrapping paper, their budding moment was about to be interrupted. Tom had been on the verge of excusing himself due to an early morning meeting when the ringing of Sarah's cell phone abruptly cut through the atmosphere.

"Chief Morgan," Sarah announced as she answered her phone, her attention shifting. Her eyes met Tom's, conveying urgency. "You're familiar with the Avalon theater downtown, right?" His nod acknowledged his understanding. "Great, thanks. Inform my officer that I'm enroute." She exchanged another glance with Tom. "County communication. There's been an incident at the movie theater. It seems to have involved some kind of colossal insect."

Without the benefit of emergency equipment, Tom deftly navigated his Ferrari through the relatively light traffic, swiftly arriving at the theater. He pulled up behind Officer Tim Moore's patrol car, his arrival marked by the distinctive engine hum of the sports car.

Presenting her badge at the vintage ticket window, Sarah and Tom gained entry into the historic movie house. Despite the old and slightly musty scent that hung in the air, the charm of the place was undeniable. The well-worn chairs, adorned with red velour cloth, exuded a sense of nostalgia, and the sight of the extended balcony above only added to the theater's timeless appeal.

Spotting Officer Moore by the side of a paramedic who was crouched down, expertly applying a wrap-around bandage to the victim's arm and hand, Sarah quickened her pace. As she approached, Moore caught sight of her and temporarily stepped away from the paramedic's side, making his way toward her. The familiar nod of greeting from Tom confirmed his recognition of the situation, a silent acknowledgment that Tom was indeed well-acquainted with many of the town's residents and police personnel.

"What's the situation?" Sarah inquired, her tone focused and alert. Officer Moore relayed the details, his eyes fixed on the unfolding events. "The victim, Annette Hartman, and her husband were seated just where you see them. She felt a sensation crawling up her leg, and when she attempted to brush it off, the creature's pincers clamped onto her hand, gripping tightly.

In the panic, she screamed, and the creature dropped to the floor. As she raised her hand, her husband noticed the blood, and he immediately began calling for assistance. Chaos erupted as others in the theater reacted with alarm, fleeing in a screaming frenzy. Strangely, aside from the victim, no one else seems to have actually witnessed the creature."

Sarah waited until after the paramedic departed to interview the witness further. "Hello, I'm so sorry for your injury. I'm Chief Sarah Morgan. Do you feel like answering just a few more questions?"

Annette's eyes held a mix of terror and disbelief as she recounted the creature's features. "It was like a nightmare come to life," Annette's voice quivered. "Long, segmented body, dark and glistening, almost like polished obsidian. It was almost three feet long. Dozens of pairs of legs, bright red, moving in eerie synchrony as it scuttled. Its pincers, sharp and sinister, clamped onto my hand like a vice. And the eyes..."

Annette's voice trailed off, haunted by the memory. "The eyes were the worst. They glowed with this otherworldly light, like fiery embers set in its hideous face. I'll never forget those eyes." Sarah's expression remained serious as she absorbed the gruesome details. This monstrous creature sounded like a grotesque hybrid of a centipede and a nightmare.

Her mind raced, trying to reconcile the surreal description with any known species. This was a challenge unlike any she had faced before, a creature that seemed beyond the realm of reason and yet was frighteningly real to the victim who had endured its attack.

Then it struck Sarah – a memory triggered by Officer Tim Moore's background investigation report. She remembered that he had an artistic inclination, though not professionally. It was a realization that could prove invaluable in this situation.

Stepping closer to Tim, Sarah presented a proposal, her voice charged with a sense of urgency. His eyes lit up with enthusiasm as he eagerly agreed to her plan. Leaving the theater briefly, he returned clutching a sketchbook. Sarah could glimpse a few of his previous drawings as he flipped through, before settling on a blank page.

As he prepared to put pencil to paper, Tim fired a series of questions at Annette. His focus was unwavering, a dedicated effort to extract every possible detail about the creature from her description. With each query, his hand moved swiftly, translating the spoken details into visual form. Gradually, lines took shape, capturing the grotesque essence of the monster that had struck terror into the heart of the theater. The creature emerged from the tip of his pencil, embodying the surreal qualities Annette had struggled to put into words. The sketch evolved, and with every stroke, the monstrous features became more defined, the chilling eyes more vivid.

Sarah watched in anticipation, her admiration for Tim's artistic skill growing with each line he drew. The page transformed into a macabre masterpiece, a creature that transcended the boundaries of reality and embodied the essence of nightmare. As the final touches were added, Sarah found herself staring at the unsettling image that had emerged from Tim's talent, a haunting portrayal of the monstrosity that had disrupted the theater.

CHAPTER

NINETEEN

S EATED ONCE AGAIN in the confines of Tom's car, a moment of respite allowed Sarah to collect her thoughts. The weight of the situation pressed down on her, and she drew in a deep breath, as if attempting to imbibe a sense of calm from the air around her. As she exhaled slowly, the tension seemed to ease, if only momentarily.

"In my career," Sarah began, her voice carrying a mix of contemplation and a hint of disbelief, "I've delved into cases involving fathers who committed the unthinkable – wiping out their entire families. I've unraveled the chilling stories of mothers who, in the darkest corners of their minds, sought to end the lives of their own children within the confines of a bathtub. These were horrors grounded in the realm of human emotion and desperation, no matter how unfathomable they may have been."

She paused, her gaze unfocused as she grappled with the words she was about to utter. "But what we're facing now, it's something beyond the scope of anything I've encountered before." The enormity of the situation seemed to hang heavy in the air. "A creature, born of some nightmarish amalgamation of the real and the unreal, haunting the very fabric of our town. It's unsettling, Tom, because this is a kind of horror that challenges not just the realm of the rational, but the very boundaries of what we consider possible."

Sarah's words held a mixture of astonishment, trepidation, and a sense of resignation. She turned her gaze to Tom, her expression a mirror of her thoughts. "Stunned, Tom. That's the only word that truly captures how I feel right now. Stunned by the fact that, even with all my years in law enforcement, I find myself standing on the precipice of something that defies explanation. And as a chief of police, my role has shifted from upholding the law to unraveling the inexplicable."

In a moment of shared vulnerability, Tom extended his arm to envelop Sarah in a comforting embrace. Unexpectedly, Sarah's response diverged from the anticipated, her emotions taking the reins as she pressed her lips to Tom's in a lingering and intimate kiss. The unexpected passion ignited a fire between them, and the kiss, intense and unanticipated, bridged the gap between them.

The embrace grew more fervent as Sarah's arms tightened around Tom, her fervor mirroring his own. Within the heated embrace, unspoken emotions seemed to dance between them, a dance of longing, desire, and an unspoken understanding that transcended mere word. It was as if in that moment, the boundaries that had been separating them, had dissolved, and what remained was the raw, undeniable connection they shared.

"Take me home," Sarah breathed, her voice laden with an undercurrent of intimacy that left no room for misinterpretation. It was a declaration that resonated with both of them, a shared desire that extended beyond mere physical proximity. In her words, the promise of a deeper connection hung in the air, an understanding that they were about to embark on a journey that would be physical and into the realm of the emotional and the intimate.

The next morning, Sarah felt movement in her new bed. She turned over and saw Tom, with his arm elevating his head, smiling down on her. "Good morning, Chief Morgan," he said, followed by a kiss on her forehead.

"Good morning to you, reporter Tom Scott," she greeted, her tone playful. Turning to meet his gaze, she discovered that he was already displaying a noticeable excitement. "Oh, what do we have here?" Sarah quipped, a mischievous glint in her eye as she playfully laid her hand on his aroused state.

Chuckling softly, Tom responded, "I'm not entirely sure. Given that you're the Chief of Police, perhaps you should conduct a thorough investigation."

The playful exchange had set them slightly behind schedule, and as a result of her unexpected "encounter" with Tom, Sarah found herself arriving at her office later than planned. The whirlwind of thoughts and the lingering effects of their playful interaction combined to clutter her mind with a list of action items for the day ahead.

"Sandy," Sarah called out as she moved with a sense of purpose toward her office. "Does the junior college you attend offer any courses in zoology or biology?"

"Absolutely," Sandy replied promptly. "I actually took a zoology course last semester. My professor was Daniel Joseph."

"Great," Sarah nodded, a plan taking shape in her mind. "Reach out to the college and see if you can obtain his contact information. If they happen to refuse, find out the necessary procedures for me to get in touch with him directly. Let them know it's a pressing police matter. And yes, use your charm, Sandy."

A short while later, Sandy approached Sarah's desk, placing a slip of paper before her. The handwritten digits on it represented Professor Joseph's cell phone number. Sandy flashed a playful wink as she did so. "Consider my charm deployed," she quipped, her grin suggesting that her persuasive tactics had indeed yielded results.

"You're destined to become an exceptional policewoman, my dear," she complimented warmly.

Sarah arrived punctually for her appointment with Professor Joseph, his college office a confined space barely larger than her own department's breakroom. A man in his sixties, he stood on the shorter side, his balding head crowned with a gray mustache. He wore an outdated herringbone sports jacket that carried the lingering scent of cigarette smoke, matched with a pristine white shirt without a tie.

A soft knock preceded Sarah's entrance, and she was granted permission to step inside. Presenting her badge, she watched as the professor's casual brush-off seemed to question the purpose of her visit. "What could an underpaid college professor possibly offer the Chief of Police of Raven's Hollow?" he mused aloud.

Choosing brevity over detailed explanation, Sarah reached into her notebook, withdrawing a copy of Officer Moore's sketch depicting the creature responsible for the movie theater attack the previous night. The drawing captured the essence of the creature's unsettling features.

"Professor, based on your expertise, what sort of creature or insect do you think this might be?" Sarah inquired, her tone a mix of curiosity and anticipation.

Joseph leaned in, examining the sketch closely as Sarah presented it. "Could you provide me with some additional details?" he requested, his gaze still fixated on the drawing. "Perhaps an estimate of its size and weight."

Recalling the victim's description, Sarah responded, "The individual who encountered it described it as being approximately three feet in length. Unfortunately, they weren't able to estimate its weight."

Joseph continued to scrutinize the image, his silence conveying his focused contemplation. Abruptly, he swiveled in his chair, his attention drawn to a row of books on a nearby shelf. Rifling through them with a determined air, he soon found the relevant page he sought. Reversing his course, he returned to his desk, placing the book down in front of Sarah with a flourish, the pages opened to reveal a pertinent passage and picture.

Joseph's fingers gently traced the lines of the sketch, his gaze shifting between the drawing and the pages of the open book before him. After a contemplative pause, he began to speak, his voice carrying a weight of authority mixed with academic enthusiasm.

"From what I can gather," he started, his eyes never leaving the sketch, "this creature bears a striking resemblance to a particular type of arthropod known as the Giant Centipede. They're ancient creatures, belonging to the class Chilopoda.

Giant Centipedes are known for their elongated, segmented bodies, often reaching lengths of up to three feet or more. While their appearance can vary somewhat, your depiction captures their defining features quite accurately."

As he spoke, Joseph's fingers flipped through the pages of the open book, revealing detailed illustrations that mirrored the characteristics in the sketch. "These creatures possess a multitude of legs, each segment bearing a pair, usually ranging from 15 to 177 pairs depending on the species. The legs themselves are adorned with bristles that provide sensory input, aiding in navigation and detecting prey."

He glanced at the drawing again before returning to the open book, tapping a detailed illustration that depicted a Giant Centipede in its natural habitat. "Giant Centipedes are predators, known for their venomous bite. Each pair of legs on the front segments bears venomous claws, capable of injecting paralyzing toxins into their prey.

The size of this creature you've depicted fits the profile, and its reported behavior – the ambush-style attack, swift movement, and the pincer-like appendages – all align with the modus operandi of a Giant Centipede. I'm just surprised your victim was not envenomated".

Joseph's gaze lifted from the book, his eyes meeting Sarah's as he concluded, "If I were to hazard a guess, Chief Morgan, this could indeed be a Giant Centipede. A creature of considerable prowess and natural weaponry, it certainly matches the details provided."

CHAPTER

TWENTY

S EEKING SOLITUDE AND a respite from her
hunger pangs, Sarah made a stop at a Subway
sandwich shop. The rushed morning had left her
with no time to share breakfast with Tom in her new
home, but the memory of that thought managed to
coax a smile onto her lips.

Seated at a table, she eagerly dug into her 6-inch
turkey and Swiss cheese sub, satisfying her appetite.
Amid the bites, she retrieved her trusty spiral notebook,
a tool that had become her partner in deciphering the
intricacies of the case.

After a contemplative pause, she penned a giant
question mark, symbolizing the lingering uncertainty.
The central query that had taken up residence in her
mind found its place on the page: *What connection
could a giant centipede possibly have to the case of a
kidnapped woman, her spleen removed?* The absurdity
of the thought briefly amused her, but she pressed on,
jotting down the main question.

As she chewed on her sandwich, Sarah's pen continued its dance across the paper. *Was the perpetrator attempting to incorporate the centipede into the victim's body?* The notion seemed grotesque and bizarre, yet it clung to her thoughts. Her forehead creased with concentration, she continued, *If so, what conceivable purpose could such a twisted act serve?*

Glancing at her watch, Sarah noted that Mary Ellen was still on-duty for the Day Shift. As she drove back to the station, she reached out to Sandy, instructing her to arrange a meeting with Mary Ellen.

Arriving at the station, Sarah found Mary Ellen waiting in the lobby. "Hello, Chief. You wanted to see me?" Mary Ellen's voice trembled slightly, betraying a hint of nervousness.

"Yes," Sarah replied, her tone composed. She gestured for Mary Ellen to follow her into her office. As they entered, Mary Ellen shut the door behind them and took a seat, her unease palpable.

"Mary Ellen, I'm not sure if you were aware, but I make it a point to review the background reports of my staff," Sarah began, her demeanor professional. Mary Ellen shifted in her chair, a sign of her discomfort.

"I noticed that you were pursuing nursing studies, but then you dropped out. Can you share why that happened?" Sarah inquired gently, her expression understanding.

Mary Ellen hesitated before responding, her nerves evident. "I suppose I just grew tired of school," she offered, her voice wavering.

Sarah continued, her gaze steady. "But it seems you were close to completing your studies and preparing for the NCLEX-RN exam."

Taking a deep breath, Mary Ellen seemed to gather her thoughts, her nervousness persisting. "My father was a doctor, and from a young age, I aspired to become one too; a surgeon. I excelled academically in high school and even earned a college scholarship."

"Initially, I was doing exceptionally well in my studies until I met my soon-to-be husband," Mary Ellen continued, her tone tinged with a mix of regret and nostalgia. "He was a pre-law student. Life took its course, and I became pregnant. Unfortunately, it turned out to be an ectopic pregnancy."

Mary Ellen's voice trembled slightly as she explained the medical condition. "An ectopic pregnancy occurs when the embryo implants outside the uterus, often in a fallopian tube. It's a dangerous situation that requires immediate intervention. I experienced pain and bleeding, and I had to undergo a procedure to remove the embryo for my own safety."

She paused, her eyes distant as she recalled that difficult time. "The stress of the situation, combined with our studies, strained our relationship. We decided to divorce, and with it went my dreams of medical school. Nursing became a compromise, but it never fulfilled my desire to become a doctor. Joining the police force was a surprise to my family and friends, a way to forge a different path."

As Mary Ellen's story unfolded, Sarah listened with empathy, recognizing the underlying emotions that had shaped her choices and journey.

"Mary Ellen, based on your medical knowledge, far superior to mine, I want to ask you some questions that are baffling me. Our homicide victim, Mrs. Thompson, as well as five other victims in surrounding jurisdictions, had their spleens removed. If that is not bizarre enough, last night a woman was attacked in the Avalon movie theater by what a zoology professor has described as a giant centipede. Do you have any guesses as to number one, why a suspect would remove a person's spleen? And, even more fantastic, can you think of why a sick person would want to insert a centipede into a person's back?"

Mary Ellen proceeded to answer the two questions. "Spleens are strange organs, located on the upper-left side of the abdomen behind the stomach. They're about the size and shape of an orange wedge, if the orange was squishy and full of blood. They're relatively fragile, and because they contain so much blood, injuries can become serious." She took a pause before continuing.

"In ancient Greek and medieval medicine, few body parts were more crucial than the spleen. People believed that the spleen was responsible for making "black bile," one of the four humors that needed to be kept in balance to stay healthy. If a spleen made too much black bile, it would make someone sad or depressed. But the spleen also cleansed the bile, so it was associated with happiness and laughter."

"We know that while you're still a fetus, the spleen makes red blood cells. And as an adult, the spleen acts as a garbage can, filtering out damaged blood cells and platelets. But you can live with some old broken blood cells, so if you injured your spleen in the 1950s, doctors wouldn't waste time trying to stitch it up. They'd cut it out in a splenectomy and send you on your way."

"But modern imaging technology has left us with a different picture of the spleen, realizing that it has a role in the immune system. Blood slows down as it passes through the spleen, which gives the immune system time to recognize and make antibodies for certain types of bacteria."

"So, could the spleen be considered like other organs for harvesting?" Sarah asked

"Perhaps, but I have never heard about that. There are so many advances and discoveries in medicine that my dad spent his leisurely hours reading medical journals after medical journals. Now, as far as your centipede question, that is just weird."

CHAPTER

TWENTY-ONE

FTER EXPRESSING HER gratitude to
Mary Ellen for sharing her story, Sarah's
attention was drawn to the shift change taking
place in the station. As the day shift transitioned
to the swing shift, she found herself multitasking,
jotting down a reminder to implement a pass-down
book system. This way, crucial information could
seamlessly flow from one shift to the next. However,
her train of thought was abruptly interrupted by the
ringing of her cell phone. Glancing at the screen, she
saw Tom's name.

"Hello, Mr. Reporter. How's your day shaping up?"
she quipped, a friendly tone in her voice.

"Sarah, it's business-related," Tom's voice carried a
note of seriousness. "They've discovered a decomposed
body, likely the kidnapped teenager from Dayton. I
figured you should be in the loop." Grateful for the
timely update, Sarah thanked Tom for the information
and ended the call.

Without hesitation, she dialed Jim's number, the Chief of Police in Dayton. He picked up after the second ring, his voice busy yet receptive.

"Jim, I know you're swamped, but I just heard about the discovery of your kidnapped victim. I have two questions for you: Was the victim's spleen removed, and was she mute?" Sarah's inquiries were direct and to the point.

Jim's response was swift, confirming both questions with a simple "yes" to each. The exchange of information was concise, a testament to the professional rapport they shared.

The following morning, Sandy was taken aback to discover Sarah already settled in her office. Perched on a short ladder, Sarah was meticulously completing the installation of a sizable wall-mounted whiteboard. Intrigued, Sandy couldn't help but inquire, "What's brewing, Chief?"

Sarah paused in her task and looked down at Sandy, a determined glint in her eyes. "You know how they say some people are visual learners?" She gestured towards the expansive whiteboard. "There's an overwhelming amount of information regarding these homicides. I need to see it all laid out before me, visually, so I can gain a comprehensive perspective. I believe the key to solving these cases is right in front of us, but it's been eluding me. Maybe by putting it all up here, I can finally see the connections."

As Sandy headed to prepare the coffee, she was met with a surprise: Sarah had beaten her to it. Not only that, but a spread of bagels and cream cheese was neatly laid out. "Looks like you've got the bagel situation under control, Chief!" Sandy called out with a grin.

Sarah's voice echoed from the kitchen, "Consider them a breakfast treat!"

Engrossed in her task, Sarah dedicated the better part of an hour to meticulously transcribing the essential details of all six homicides, including that of Mrs. Thompson. In her quest for the missing puzzle piece that could potentially crack the case wide open, Sarah was met with repeated disappointments as each lead she pursued failed to yield the breakthrough she sought.

A knock on her slightly ajar office door drew her attention, and she spotted Chelsea standing there, holding a bag of food from Taco Bell. Chelsea's easy grin was infectious. "Hey, Chief, it's Taco Tuesday. Care to take a break and indulge?"

Sarah's eyes lifted from her notes, a smile playing on her lips as she welcomed the idea. "Sounds like a plan, Doctor. Let's have a break."

As they both ate their tacos and drank their sodas, Chelsea was amazed at the amount of information Sarah had on the white board. "Did you hear?" Sarah asked. "Dayton Police found the body of the missing teenage girl early this morning. She was badly decomposed but the Chief over at Dayton confirmed she was mute and had her spleen removed."

"When I return to the office, I'll reach out to my colleague over there and have her fax me the autopsy report. I'll make sure to forward it to you promptly," Chelsea assured, her tone focused. However, her gaze shifted to the expansive whiteboard in the room. "Although, it seems you've got quite a handful with this." She motioned toward the whiteboard, where a web of information was neatly organized. "Do you have any substantial leads on our suspect?"

Sarah's expression turned rueful. "Not quite yet. If anything, the cases are becoming more perplexing as we delve deeper."

Curiosity sparkled in Chelsea's eyes. "In what way?" she probed, leaning in slightly.

Taking a moment to gather her thoughts, Sarah recounted the unsettling attack at the movie theater involving the colossal centipede. She shared the murmurs circulating among the citizens about the enigmatic "Fearmonger," adding, "I just have this instinct that the answers we need are somewhere here on this whiteboard, waiting to be connected."

As the remnants of their meal were tidied up, the familiar sound of Sarah's cell phone interrupted the moment. "Chief Morgan speaking. How can I assist you?" Her tone shifted as the conversation progressed. "Ah, hey there. Yes, I did reach out to the Dayton Chief, and he indeed confirmed my suspicions. That's interesting to hear."

Chelsea picked up on the intimate nature of the call and respectfully excused herself with a subtle wave. She mouthed a promise to notify Sarah if any new information came up.

Over time, Medussa had skillfully adapted to her environment, drawing sustenance from the sewage that flowed through the intricate network of sewer systems crisscrossing Raven's Hollow. Her size had undergone a remarkable transformation, now stretching nearly six feet in length. While her palate certainly leaned towards the concoctions supplied by the twisted mind of Dr. Sinclair, she had managed to maintain her resilience and survival instincts in the untamed wild outside the confines of the laboratory.

Feeding off the waste and filth that the sewer systems offered, Medussa's evolution was a testament to her ability to adapt and thrive in even the most challenging conditions. She was no longer solely reliant on the specialized sustenance created by Dr. Sinclair, which had initially nurtured her growth. Instead, her forays into the sewers had equipped her with an alternate means of sustenance, allowing her to sustain her size and strength.

CHAPTER

TWENTY-TWO

THE CRISP AUTUMN air carried the excitement of the homecoming football game between Raven's Hollow and Riverside High school. The bleachers were alive with not only fans adoring their team's colors, but also with the cheers and the rhythmic clapping of hands.

On Raven's Hollow side of the field, colors of red and black, while across the field, Riverside High fans displayed black and gold.

Mayor Wadsworth, never missing an event where he could engage with voters, was sitting in the bleachers at the fifty-year line wearing his signature grin, among the enthusiastic townspeople, a proud supporter of the home team.

In the midst of the fanfare, a dark presence slithered beneath the bleachers, unnoticed by the revelers. Medussa, the Tingler, with its spine-tingling malevolence, inched its way forward. Its intent was clear: to target the legs of unsuspecting attendees, causing shivers of fear to ripple through the crowd.

Amid the buzz, Sarah stood at the edge of the bleachers, her eyes scanning the scene for any signs of trouble. A sudden commotion caught her attention. Officer Mary Ellen Statton was whispering urgently into her cell phone, her brow furrowed in concern.

Sarahs' instincts kicked in, and she moved closer to eavesdrop on the conversation.

"We need to be careful, Mary Ellen whispered, her voice tinged with urgency. She's going to put the pieces together."

As if sensing danger, Medussa hesitated. It poised itself for a strike, its tendrils quivering with anticipation. Just as its grip was about to close around a leg, the crowd erupted in a collective scream. The kick-off had sent shockwaves of excitement through the air, scattering the tingler's intended victims.

Sarah and Mary Ellen continued to watch the crowd and a Raven's Hollow player made a great run back. Under the bleachers, the tingler retreated back into the shadows. As the game continued, the pulsating energy of the crowd overshadowed the lingering sense of unease.

Dr. Sinclair paced back and forth in his dimly lit study, his face etched with a mix of frustration and anxiety. The recent developments were a cause for concern, and the call he was about to receive would either ease his worries or escalate his fears.

The phone on his desk buzzed, and he reached for it with a sense of trepidation. He pressed the receiver to his ear, listening intently to the voice on the other end. The words were succinct, delivered with a cold, calculated tone that sent a shiver down Sinclair's spine.

"They're getting close. They know more than you think. We must meet and decide what to do." The line then went dead.

Sinclair's grip on the phone tightened as he absorbed the weight of the message. He had known that the web of deception was growing thinner by the day, but hearing it confirmed in the phone conversation sent a jolt of panic through him. He needed more time, more secrecy, to ensure that his plans remained intact.

He paced the room, his mind a whirlwind of strategies and countermeasures. The police's progress was relentless, their pursuit relentless, and he knew that the game was reaching its critical point.

As he glanced out the window, the moonlight cast eerie shadows across the room. Sinclair made a decision. If he was to safeguard his experiments, his legacy, he would need to take drastic measures. With a heavy sigh, he turned his attention to a hidden compartment beneath his desk, where a collection of files and notes were stashed away.

The anticipation in Raven's Hollow was palpable as the grand opening of Dreamscape, the new virtual reality park, approached. The entire town buzzed with excitement, as both residents and visitors eagerly awaited the unveiling of this cutting-edge entertainment hub.

GARY J. ROSE

Sarah stood in front of the entrance, taking in the futuristic architecture and the crowd had gathered. It reminded her of Sci/fi conventions held in the past in LA, where attendees tried to outdo each other with their costumes. Instead, these people showed up dressed as their avatar.

The sleek glass façade of Dreamscape reflected the vibrant lights of the surrounding area, creating an illusion of being in a world beyond reality. Inside, state-of-the-art VR technology promised to transport participants to realms of their wildest imaginations.

As the ribbon-cutting ceremony commenced, Sarah watched as the scissors sliced through the ribbon, and the doors swung open. A rush of paid customers streamed inside, their faces a mixture of awe and wonder. Within the expansive interior, pods and stations were set up, each offering a unique virtual experience.

Sarah wandered through the park, observing people immersed in various virtual worlds. Some were soaring through the skies, while others battled mythical creatures in epic landscapes. The excitement was contagious, and the energy infectious. Yet, even in the midst of the spectacle, Sarah couldn't shake off the shadows that lingered in the corners of her mind.

The park's creators spared no expense, boasting the latest advancements in VR technology. Sarah found herself drawn to the station where participants were navigating through a futuristic city, their movements

170

translating seamlessly into the digital realm. She watched as a young woman laughed with delight as she scaled virtual skyscrapers.

Though the festivities were captivating, Sarah's police instincts remained sharp. She observed the interactions, the subtle exchanges, and the emotions that played across participant's faces. Dreamscape might have been a haven of entertainment, but she knew that beneath the surface, there were stories waiting to be uncovered.

As the day progressed, she saw Mayor Wadsworth follow the executives of Dreamscape like a loyal dog, hoping to be petted occasionally. Sarah continued her exploration of Dreamscape, her mind, a whirlwind of thoughts and suspicions. This high-tech haven was the embodiment of Raven's Hollow's aspirations for a brighter future, but she couldn't help but wonder if the darkness that had gripped the town would find a way to seep into this realm of dreams.

CHAPTER

TWENTY-THREE

D AYS AFTER THE grand opening of
Dreamscape, Sarah found herself immersed
in her role as Chief of Police. The excitement
of the virtual reality park had settled into a constant
hum in the background of her thoughts. She had
more pressing matter to attend to.

Sitting at her desk, Sarah flipped through the files
and reports that had accumulated. Among them was
the ongoing investigation into the tingler incidents.
She glanced up as Sandy entered her office.

"Chief, got a minute?" she asked

Sarah gestured for her to take a seat. "Of course,
Sandy. What's on your mind?"

Sandy cleared her throat, her expression a mixture
of anticipation and determination. "I wanted to thank
you for promoting me to police officer. I'm excited to
take on this new role."

Sarah smiled warmly. "You've earned it, Sandy.
Your dedication and commitment to the department

haven't gone unnoticed. We're lucky to have you on the team."

Sandy's gratitude was evident in her eyes. "Thank you Chief. I won't let you down."

"We have another recruit to select before training can commence," Sarah reminder her. "But, I'm confident you'll do well at the police academy."

Sandy nodded, her enthusiasm undeterred. "I'm ready for the challenge."

After Sandy departed from Sarah's office, she jotted down a reminder to herself. She needed to publish two vacancies for veteran officers to apply to the Raven's Hollow Police Department to fill the void left by Sandy's departure and contribute to street coverage. With budget concerns in mind, having reliable officers in place was crucial.

In a second note, she urged herself to begin establishing connections with diverse city council members. This strategic move aimed to secure allies who could support her during budget discussions, ensuring she had influential voices on her side if Mayor Wadsworth's promises faltered.

Sarah's gaze now shifted to the cityscape visible through her office window. Beyond the exterior calm, she knew that Raven's Hollow held secrets, and the tingler incidents were far from resolved. She still needed to discover the one tangible piece of evidence to solve the case.

Who was Mary Ellen warning that she might put the pieces together? Mary Ellen Statton. Former nurses' candidate. Father was a doctor. Medical knowledge. Desire to be a surgeon. These were leads that had to be followed.

She spent hours delving deeper into the tingler investigation looking for anything she missed. She now realized that the answer she sought lay in the past. She called Tom at the Examiner to see if he was free for lunch. The two agreed to visit a local Burger King.

Bringing her reports along, Sarah anticipated Tom's potential delay. Seizing the opportunity, she immersed herself in the sea of papers and files, poring over the information. The more she delved into the details, the heavier her heart sank.

At last, Tom arrived, and after he placed their orders, they settled into the comfort of a corner booth. As he greeted her with an affectionate kiss—a gesture he adored—Tom inquired, "So, Chief of Police Sarah, how's the battle faring?"

A wry smile tugged at her lips, and she replied, "I'm on the verge of raising the white flag, I must admit."

"While I have something that might brighten up your day, besides me of course. I found something that might shed light on the tingler's origin. It traces back to a Dr. Warren Chapin and his assistant, Dr. David Morris. They were researching a microscopic organism that resides in the spleen, growing in size when a person experiences fear."

"Go on." Sarah said.

Tom continued after swallowing a French fry and washing it down with a sip of his soda. "When a person screams, the tingler's power diminishes. But, if the person is mute, unable to scream, the tingler becomes lethal, breaking their back and ultimately causing their death."

Sarah's mind raced, connecting the dots between this information and the series of mute victims she was aware of. "That explains the pattern of the killings. What happened to Dr. Chapin and his assistant, whatever his name was? Are they still alive?"

"Dr. Chapin died years ago. He continued his experiments using himself as a test subject. Now get this. He would inject massive amounts of LSD into his system, trying to experience intense fear and analyze how his spleen area reacted. One night he fell to his death."

"Now his assistant, Dr. David Morris, gave up his medical license years ago following the death of Dr. Chapin. He is alive but now a vegetable, needing 24/7 care."

Sarah contemplated the implications of this revelation. The tingler was not just a random threat; it had roots in a sinister experiment that spanned years and someone is continuing those experiments. She realized that to confront the tingler's menace, she would need to understand its origins and its connection to Raven's Hollow.

CHAPTER

TWENTY-FOUR

T HE MAYOR'S RESIDENCE stood as a symbol of authority and influence in Raven's Hollow. It was a place where decisions were made, and power was wielded. But, within its walls, darkness lurked, and the events that unfolded that night would forever alter the town's fate.

Mayor Wadsworth reclined in his favorite armchair, sipping a glass of expensive brandy as he basked in the afterglow of Dreamscape's success. He savored the moment of triumph, his mind preoccupied with visions of the future.

Closing his eyes, a recurring dream took over. A dream where he was having sex with his secretary, Amanda, on top of his mayor's desk. Unknown to him, a shadowy figure had entered the premises, Medussa, the Tingler, slid through a doggie door, its movements soundless and deliberate. It navigated the interior, inching its way closer to the unsuspecting mayor.

As Medussa reached the mayor's chair, its tendrils extended, encircling his throat. A sudden jolt of fear and pain surged through Mayor Wadsworth's veins, his eyes widening in terror as he realized that it was not part of a dream. He struggled, gasping for breath, but the Tingler's grip was unyielding.

Within moments, the mayor's struggle ceased, his body slumping in the chair as Medussa began to rip flesh from the throat area. Blood ran down the mayor's shirt eventually pooling on the bottom cushion. The once mighty mayor had fallen victim to the very fear he had sought to exploit for the town's benefit.

The Tingler's malevolent presence lingered in the room, a chilling reminder of its power. As its tendrils retracted, the room returned to an eerie stillness, broken only by the haunting echoes of what had transpired. Raven's Hollow had lost a leader, but the darkness that had claimed the mayor's life would not rest.

Sarah and Tom arrived at Dr. David Morris's residence, a quiet suburban home surrounded by a well-tended garden. The nurse, a kindly woman named Mrs. Peterson, greeted them at the door. She wore a gentle smile as she ushered them inside, her eyes reflecting a mixture of sympathy and the weariness that came from years of caring for a patient in need of constant attention.

"It's very nice to meet you two. We don't get many visitors," Mrs. Thompson said in a soft voice, leading them down a softly lit corridor. "Dr. Morris's condition is quite delicate, but he's aware of your visit."

They stepped into a room filled with medical equipment, softly beeping monitors, and the unmistakable scent of sterile surroundings. Dr. Morris lay on a hospital bed, tubes and wires extending from his body like lifelines. An intricate network of machinery sustained his existence, including a ventilator that provided the breath he could not take on his own.

Sarah's heart sank at the sight. It was clear that extracting any coherent information from him was an impossible endeavor. His eyes, though open, seemed distant and unfocused.

The nurse glanced at them, understanding their unspoken thoughts. "I'm afraid he can't communicate in the conventional sense," she said gently. "But if you need a moment with him, please take it."

Respecting the nurse's offer, Sarah and Tom approached Dr. Morris's bedside. They exchanged a somber glance before shifting their attention to the notes and files strewn across a nearby desk. The material appeared to be a mix of medical records and research documents.

Gaining a nod of approval from the nurse, they set about sifting through the scattered papers. Among the meticulously kept notes and documents, they unearthed a trail of references to Dr. Warren Chapin's macabre experiments centered around tinglers. As their eyes roved over the text, a tapestry of understanding began to unfurl.

Piece by piece, the puzzle found its form as they absorbed the chilling details. The writings divulged Chapin's autopsy reports on deceased convicts—men who had met their demise either naturally or through the iron hand of a death sentence. From these cadavers, Chapin had extracted his unending supply of research subjects, performing grisly surgeries to excise their spleens and delve into the depths of experimentation.

The concept of the Tingler emerged from the shadows of his notes—a malevolent entity capable of orchestrating death through the weapon of fear. Each phrase they absorbed deepened the darkness of Chapin's pursuits, the quiet and controlled environment of his study now haunted by the specter of his relentless curiosity.

But it was the final note that sent shivers down their spines. A handwritten entry, penned by Dr. David Morris himself, revealed the shocking twist. As his health declined, he had sought the assistance of another neurosurgeon, Dr. Adrian Sinclair.

The implications of this revelation were profound. Sarah and Tom exchanged a wide-eyed look, realizing that this Dr. Sinclair's involvement in the case went deeper than they had ever imagined. The quest for answers had taken an unforeseen turn, and the shadows that enveloped Raven's Hollow seemed to stretch even further.

As Sarah steered her police car, Tom conducted a swift Internet search. The results painted a picture of Dr. Adrian Sinclair's past. Once upon a time, he had occupied a prominent position as a distinguished neuroscientist within a renowned medical university. However, a cloud of mystery shrouded his trajectory, as he was inexplicably removed from his position. Inquiries into the reasons behind his dismissal were met with the usual refrain of 'personnel matters remain confidential.

In the confined space of the car, the information they uncovered raised more questions than answers. The enigma surrounding Sinclair deepened, casting a shadow over his credentials and intentions. The pieces of the puzzle were beginning to come together, leading them down a twisted path that held more secrets than they could have anticipated.

Just as they were engrossed in their investigation of Dr. Sinclair, Sarah received a call for assistance. A creature had breached Dreamscape, attacking participatns as they navigated alternate worlds.

"Let's go," Sarah declared, determination hardening her resolve. "We can't let the tingler's terror continue."

As they raced to the scene, Sarah's heart pounded with a mix of anticipation and dread. She knew that the showdown with the tingler was inevitable, that they were racing against time to put an end to its reign of fear.

CHAPTER

TWENTY-FIVE

SARAH'S ARRIVAL AT Dreamscape was marked by a pounding heart, her senses heightened as she surveyed the disarray unfolding before her eyes. The once vibrant atmosphere had devolved into chaos, and her primary focus was locating Officer Statton amidst the turmoil. Panic and fear etched themselves across the faces of participants who, only moments ago, had been immersed in the illusory embrace of virtual worlds that had now morphed into haunting nightmares. The tingler's malevolent presence had shattered their sense of security, leaving them adrift in a sea of terror.

Navigating through the tumult, Sarah pressed forward, undeterred by the frenzy that enveloped her. Her determination to confront the tingler was unwavering, a flicker of resolve amidst the chaos. As she pushed through the pandemonium, she witnessed a trail of individuals emerging from the main building, their arms and hands marked with streaks of crimson, their legs mangled from desperate escapes. The mayhem was the handiwork of Medusa—the entity whose unleashed power had transformed the sanctuary of Dreamscape into a nightmare realm.

Sarah's steps quickened, driven by a potent mix of urgency and a steadfast desire to halt the escalating horror.

As she rounded a corner, her eyes widened in alarm. The creature, with three-quarters of its 9' body stretching upwards, withered is tendrils with violent motions, snapping at anything that moved. It focused on those participants who were trapped in a virtual environment.

Without hesitation, Sarah drew her weapon and aimed with steady precision as Tom looked on. The tingler's grotesque form recoiled as she fired, the shot piercing through its darkness. The creature let out a chilling screech and started moving rapidly towards Sarah and Tom. Sarah fired rapidly emptying her 9 mm. As she was preparing to replace her clip with new ammunition, the tingler shook violently before finally being extinguished.

"You did it Sarah. You stopped it," an excited Tom shouted. Sarah knew that the scars the tingler had left behind would linger. Sarah with the aid of Mary Ellen, kept the crowd back from the dead creature. More and more sirens from ambulances and the fire department could be heard in the background.

Sarah looked at Tom. "We still need to find out how this all started, and who is behind it."

As if on cue, Sarah's radio crackled to life. County dispatch reported an incident at the mayor's house. With a shared glance, Sarah and Tom knew that their investigation was far from over. Sarah called Sandy, telling her to order the two swing shift officers to come in early and assist Mary Ellen at Dreamscape. Activating her emergency equipment, Sarah and Tom rushed to the mayor's house, the weight of their discoveries hung heavy in the air. The tingler's reign of fear and terror had ended, but the web of intrigue that had enveloped Raven's Hollow was far from untangled.

Arriving at the mayor's residence, a maid met them at an opened front door. She led the two into the mayor's home office. The scene before them was grim – a lifeless body slumped in a chair, with chucks of flesh removed from the throat area. A haunting echo of the tingler's touch. The mayor's demise was a stark reminder that even those in power were not immune to the darkness that had plagued the town.

Sarah examined the scene, her mind racing with questions. Why had the tingler targeted the mayor? What was the connection between the mayor and the tingler's presence? Would she ever have those questions answered?

We need to get to this Dr. Sinclair's house ASAP. I have a bad feeling about this," Sarah said. She called

Sandy, telling her to have one of the two swing shift officers stand by at the mayor's residence, securing the scene. She also said to call in Officer Kneale from grave yard. God it would have been nice if she had realistic staff. Your death, Mr. Mayor, will go a long way to fulfilling that need, she thought.

Sinclair found himself preoccupied with the task of nourishing Lamia, the appellation he had assigned to the tingler procured from the speechless adolescent girl. Drawing from Greek mythology, Lamia represented a malevolent entity with a woman's torso seamlessly merging into the serpentine lower body. The legend held that she had an appetite for consuming children, thus embodying dread and terror. Sinclair believed this name aptly suited the centipede-like creature's nature.

As he provided sustenance to the tingler, which seemed to savor its nourishment, Sinclair's mind remained occupied with devising a strategy to free himself from his fellow researcher's influence. His intent was to orchestrate a scenario in which law enforcement would reach the conclusion that the unsolved cases attributed to the tingler remained unresolved.

This scheme necessitated a sacrifice, the life of Lamia, whom he intended to abandon within his collaborator's residence, thereby exposing her to police scrutiny. Yes, he mused, this course of action was imperative. It would not only permit the continuity of his research but also secure his name as a prominent figure in forthcoming medical and scientific publications.

In the midst of Sinclair's engagement with Lamia, tending to its feeding, his laboratory suddenly admitted an unexpected presence. The entrance of his co-conspirator sent a brief jolt of surprise through him, only to be swiftly replaced by a sense of ease as familiarity settled in. There was an air of camaraderie as the two shared glances, their connection underscored by their shared endeavors.

With a gracious gesture, the other researcher extended a proposal to celebrate their accomplishments thus far, producing a bottle of champagne. The clinking of glasses reverberated within the lab's walls as they raised their drinks in a toast to their collaborative research. Unbeknownst to Sinclair, treacherous intent lurked beneath the surface – a lethal poison surreptitiously introduced into the sparkling liquid via a concealed syringe.

As the glasses were lowered and the poison made its insidious impact, Sinclair's strength waned, causing him to slump to the floor in a disoriented daze. It was then that the co-conspirator's purpose became chillingly apparent. Seizing a scalpel from the cluttered desk, she methodically incised Sinclair's throat, liberating Lamia from its cage. The centipede-like creature, drawn to the scene, converged on the newly exposed area and began to feed.

Amidst the unfolding tableau, the distant wail of sirens grew more pronounced. Time seemed to compress as the co-conspirator, quick-witted and driven by urgency, seized the glasses and the bottle of poisoned champagne. A hasty exit ensued, leaving behind a scene of macabre significance.

Sarah and Tom's arrival was marked by an open side door to the laboratory – an unsettling sight that roused their apprehension. Their gaze fell upon the visceral tableau: Lamia feasting upon Sinclair's fallen form. Sarah's reaction was swift and decisive – a forceful kick that dislodged the creature, followed by a resolute gunshot that terminated its existence. A check for a pulse on Sinclair was negative.

"Gee. Do you think this ends it?" Tom asked. Sarah was about to answer when her attention was diverted to a picture on one of the walls in the lab. Sarah's heart sank.

CHAPTER

TWENTY-SIX

T HE SUN CAST long shadows as Sarah and Tom stood outside the county coroner's office. Their pursuit of truth had led them down a path of revelations and darkness, and they were prepared to confront the secrets that lay hidden within the walls of authority.

Inside the coroner's office, Sarah was met by Chelsea, the coroner herself. A sense of tension hung in the air as they exchanged glances. Sarah's resolve was unwavering as she opened her briefcase that contained a stack of evidence and files including a photograph. Before displaying them, she focused on medical examiner.

"Chelsea, we've been digging into the tingler's origins, and we know that it's tied to something much bigger," Sarah began, her voice steady. "We also know that you've been involved."

Chelsea's expression shifted from surprise to a cold, calculating gaze. "And what if I have been involved? What can you prove?"

Sarah's gaze locked onto Chelsea's eyes. "We have evidence that connects you with the tingler's creation, to its manipulation for your own agenda and that of Dr. Adrian Sinclair. You exploited power and it ends now."

"Who is this Dr. Sinclair you mentioned? I have never heard of him."

Sarah pulled out a picture she had taken off the wall of Sinclair's laboratory showing a young Chelsea with her mentor, Dr. Adrian Sinclair.

As the tension escalated, Chelsea's demeanor shifted. A manic smile spread across her face, her laughter tinged with an unsettling edge. "You think you can stop me? You think you can unravel the darkness I've woven?"

With a swift determined movement, Chelsea grabbed a scalpel from a nearby table, her actions fueled by desperation and madness. As the room erupted into chaos, the truth unveiled itself with a chilling finality.

In a heart-stopping instant, Chelsea's swift action precluded any response from Sarah or Tom. With a deft movement, she severed her carotid artery, a gush of crimson staining the autopsy room in a morbid display. Crumpling to the floor, Chelsea's life force ebbed away, leaving a jarring scene in its wake. Sarah's instincts propelled her to Chelsea's side, a desperate attempt to offer solace in the face of impending tragedy.

Amidst the haunting tableau, Chelsea's voice trembled as she whispered her last sentiments. "All I wanted was recognition for my contributions to the tingler research," her words carried a poignant weight. "I deserved acknowledgment in the publications, not just Adrian."

And with those final utterances, the room bore witness to the collision of ambition, despair, and a desperate yearning for validation, encapsulated in the fleeting moments before Chelsea's light was extinguished.

The aftermath of the confrontation with Chelsea, left a somber atmosphere that lingered over Raven's Hollow. The darkness that had gripped the town had been confronted and defeated, but the scars it had left behind were a testament to the toll it had taken.

As the days passed, Sarah found herself immersed in the tasks of rebuilding and healing. The police force worked tirelessly to restore a sense of security, and the town slowly began to mend its wounds. The shadow of the tingler's terror was fading, replaced by a collective determination to move forward.

One morning, Sarah entered the police station, now being remodeled and expanded, to find her entire staff gathered in the main room. Her heart warmed as she took in their smiles and expressions of Happy Birthday. "God, Chief, with everything going on, I was sure that you would have put the pieces together and ruin our surprise," Mary Ellen stated.

As the group sang the traditional Happy Birthday song, followed by an applause, Sarah reflected on the journey that had brought them to this point. From the discovery of the tingler's origin to the unmasking of its perpetrators, they had confronted darkness and emerged victorious. And as the town moved forward, Sarah knew that the lessons learned from their experiences would guide them toward a brighter future.

With a sense of closure and the support of her team, Sarah looked ahead. The chapter of the tingler's terror was ending, and a new chapter of healing, unity, and celebration was just beginning.

CHAPTER

TWENTY-SEVEN

THE SUN SHONE brightly over Raven's Hollow as Sarah and Tom stood among the crowd gathered outside the police academy. The air was filled with excitement and anticipation as the graduation ceremony of the new police recruits was about to begin. For Sarah this event held a special significance – it marked the culmination of a journey that had tested her resolve and strength.

Beside her, Tom's presence was a source of comfort and support. Their shared experiences had deepened their connection, and their partnership had grown into something more profound. The darkness they had confronted had only strengthened their bond, reminding them of the importance of unity in the face of adversity.

As the ceremony commenced, the graduates proudly marched in wearing their department's uniform. Their determination evident in their steps. Among them were Sandy and Sean, the new recruits who had joined the force at a critical juncture. Sarah's heart swelled with pride as she watched them, knowing that the future of Raven's Hollow was in capable hands.

Amid the applause and cheers, Sandy and Sean received their badges, a symbol of their commitment to upholding the law and protecting their community. Sarah exchanged a meaningful glance with Tom and a wink with Sandy.

After the ceremony, Sarah and Tom joined the graduates and their families in celebrating this momentous occasion. The atmosphere was one of hope and optimism, a testament to the town's ability to heal and move forward. As the sun set, casting a warm glow over the gathering, Sarah couldn't help but feel a sense of closure.

Amid the downtown streets, the proprietors of the Avalon movie theater had concluded their duties for the night, securing the building and proceeding toward their parked vehicle. The distant jingling of keys marked their departure, a gentle melody in the urban night. With their car engine humming to life, they eased into motion, leaving behind the dimly lit facade.

Yet, as the car's taillights faded into the distance, a disconcerting sound reverberated from the shadows, emanating from a storm drain nestled near the pavement's edge. The initial note was a mere murmur, a low-pitched groan that could have been dismissed as an echo of the night's stillness. But the utterance persisted, intensifying in both volume and fervor, as if the very conduit of the drain resented its containment.

From the depths of this humble drain, an eerie transformation unfolded. Unfurling with an eerie deliberation, crimson-hued antennae, sinuous and menacing, breached the drain's confines. Its' emergence was followed by a spectacle as uncanny as it was unsettling: a sleek and elongated black body, slithered its way into the moonlight. A multitude of scarlet feet, acting in eerie harmony, added to this surreal emergence, as the creature meticulously wrested itself free from the drain's grip.

Having successfully liberated itself, the creature wasted no time in asserting its presence. In an astonishing display of vitality, it contorted its form, arching over in a menacing curve that spanned nearly half its staggering length of nine feet. In a gesture that resonated with both primordial proclamation and sinister threat, the creature unleashed a snap of its mandibles, an ominous sound that reverberated through the air as if announcing to the world that the 'Tingler' had been unleashed.

MOVIE POSTERS
FOR THE FILM

TRIBUTE
TO THE CAST

VINCENT PRICE
Dr. Warren Chapin

PHILIP COOLIDGE
Ollie Higgins

PATRICIA CUTTS
Isabel Chapin

JUDITH EVELYN
Mrs. Martha Ryerson Higgins

DARRYL HICKMAN
Dr. David Morris

PAMELA LINCOLN
Lucy Stevens

DIRECTOR WILLIAM CASTLE

Castle opened the film, "The Tingler," with an on-screen warning to the audience:

"I am William Castle, the director of the motion picture you are about to see. I feel obligated to warn you that some of the sensations—some of the physical reactions which the actors on the screen will feel—will also be experienced, for the first time in motion picture history, by certain members of this audience. I say 'certain members' because some people are more sensitive to these mysterious electronic impulses than others. These unfortunate, sensitive people will at times feel a strange, tingling sensation; other people will feel it less strongly. But don't be alarmed—you can protect yourself. At any time you are conscious of a tingling sensation, you may obtain immediate relief by screaming. Don't be embarrassed about opening your mouth and letting rip with all you've got, because the person in the seat right next to you will probably be screaming too. And remember this—a scream at the right time may save your life."

"Dear reader, as I reach the end of this journey we've taken together through the pages of my novel, I want to extend my heartfelt gratitude to you. Your dedication to exploring the world I've crafted and the lives of the characters I've brought to life has been an honor for me as an author. I hope that my words have entertained, moved, and resonated with you in some way. If you enjoy my novel, I kindly ask you to consider sharing your thoughts on Amazon. com. Look up my title and post your review. Your reviews not only provide invaluable feedback but also help other readers discover the magic that lies within these pages."

Thank you,

Gary J. Rose

www.ingramcontent.com/pod-product-compliance
Lightning Source LLC
Chambersburg PA
CBHW020642260626
47157CB00008B/2878